The Fantasy Works

A Collection of Short Stories and Poems

Dennis Maulsby

Dennis Maulsby

THE FANTASY WORKS

For more information: www.neoleafpress.com

ISBN: 978-1-945663-26-0

First Edition: February 2020

Acknowledgments

Grateful acknowledgment is made to publishers of books, periodicals, and anthologies in which these poems and stories or earlier versions of them have appeared.

Stories:

Group Therapy — 2016, *Free Fire Zone*, Prolific Press.

Supermarket Takeout — 2016, *Free Fire Zone,* Prolific Press.

The Norwegian American Troll — 2019, *Winterset*, NeoLeaf Press, and 2019, *The Norwegian American Newspaper.*

Freudian Slips — 2019, Third Flatiron anthology *Hidden Histories.*

Amtrac Dream — 2015, Honorable mention, Mary Kennedy Eastham flash fiction contest.

Monkey See, Monkey Go — Recognition award from Ageless Authors.

Poems:

Grandmothers' Dance — 2012, first place award Pennsylvania Poets Society; 2012, Senior Poet's award, Angels Without Wings Foundation; and 2015, *Near Death/Near Life*, Prolific Press.

Omaha Beach — 2004, National Public Radio's *Themes & Variations* and 2015, *Near Death/Near Life*, Prolific Press.

Dennis Maulsby

Flor de la Luna II — 2015, *Near Death/Near Life*, Prolific Press.

My Asian Son — 2004, *The North American Review*; 2010, Terracotta Typewriter; and 2015, *Near Death/Near Life*, Prolific Press.

Memory of a Eurasian Working Girl — 2010, *Lyrical Iowa* and 2015, *Near Death/Near Life*, Prolific Press.

Pictures from Orbit — 2004, *Lyrical Iowa* and 2015, *Near Death/Near Life*, Prolific Press.

They're Alive, Alive ... — 2015, *Near Death/Near Life*, Prolific Press.

Kill Zone Requiem — 2017, *Iowa Informer* and 2015, *Near Death/Near Life*, Prolific Press.

The Fantasy Works
by Dennis Maulsby

Welcome to The Fantasy Works. Check out works of poetry, short stories, and novel extracts, previously published and yet-to-be-published. Read tales of war and peace, demons, and the old gods – the past forcing itself upon the present. In the following pages, you will find stories, poems, and excerpts from these books and manuscripts.

- *Free Fire Zone* (short stories published by Prolific Press in 2016) – A war veteran must find harmony with an alternate berserker personality.

- *Winterset* (short stories published by NeoLeaf Press in 2019) – A venerable small-town alcoholic priest takes on an underworld of demons, pixies, and fiends.

- *The Assisi* (unpublished novel) – This coming of age novel is set in a post- apocalyptic world two-hundred and fifty years in the future. A boy on the edge of manhood must master his psychic abilities to save human-kind from extinction.

- *Near Death/Near Life* (published by Prolific Press in 2015) – Travel to war zones and peaceful interludes far and near in a collection of prize-winning poetry.

- *The Adamson Files* (unpublished novels) – Selections from the first two books of a trilogy bring you into the ageless world of a succubus/incubus, sister and brother personalities, sharing one body.

- *The Sommelier* (unpublished novel) – The old god Dionysus and his girlfriend Terpsichore, the muse of dance, work as independent contractors for the CIA. Industrial espionage and assassination are their specialties.

- *The House de Gracie* (to be released by NeoLeaf Press in 2020) – A dying Major Hugh de Gracie, the prodigal son, returns to his ancestral home in New York's Adirondacks. His once rejected family will finally disclose their secrets. Their five-hundred-year-old chateau is a living plant and they its symbiotes.

Stories from *The Adamson Files* and *The Adamson Files: Normandie*

The Adamson Files: It's contemporary New York City. Mixing every day with the normal human inhabitants of the Big Apple are creatures of myth and legend. Besides being brother and sister, Lilith and Keean are a succubus/incubus, two demons — one male, one female — cursed for eternity to inhabit one body. They morph back and forth between male and female aspects as needed for their seductions. The carnal relations allow them to steal the life force of their victims to keep themselves young. The pair is over 350,000 years old and carry the burden of countless historical moments. Recognized as malevolent demons by the priests of a centuries-old department of the Catholic Church, they are marked for destruction.

THE SERIAL KILLER MEETS A DEMON

Lilith tried to ease the alcohol-drug-induced headache by maintaining a low level of meditation. From how things were progressing, she would need a much deeper physical disconnect from this level of reality soon. Testing the bonds and finding them too strong to break, she felt embarrassed. A thought crossed her mind: evidently living a long time did not necessarily make you *that* much smarter.

McClary & Associates Private Detectives had been hired by rich distraught parents to find their missing daughter. The police were having no luck other than believing they had the worst serial killer in fifty years picking off women frequenting the numerous bars of the Big Apple. And the daughter might possibly be one of the victims. A brainstorming session consisting of their partner Joe, a retired NYC police officer, and herself had spotted consistencies in place and times of abduction.

The killer worked off a popular Internet list of the top fifty bars in the city. Once a week, he picked a bar off the list via the multiplication table of fives. The last three missing women had attended the fifth bar on the list, the tenth, and the fifteenth. All abductions took place on a Wednesday night. Hump day, when young singles tired of the workplace, begin to build up their hopes for the coming weekend.

Lilith had agreed to visit bar twenty and look for suspects. She had turned down Joe's offer to accompany her as backup. No sense in giving the killer two chances to uncover the trap. He offered a snub nose colt .38 for her purse. As a demon succubus, she had enough natural weapons.

If anything, she had felt over-armed. But even the gods can suffer hubris, Lilith remembered *pride goeth before a fall*. The musty rotting fug of an abandoned old house, damp and cold – the current reality.

And there she was, bare-ass naked, ankles and knees duct-taped to two of a table's legs, which were firmly secured to the floor with 'L' shaped angle irons. The rest of her stripped goose-bumped body bent facedown over the wooden top, hands bound at the wrists pinned beneath her body. Her neck hanging off the far end of the table was tied with wire to an eyebolt set into the floor. Plastic sheeting flowed underneath her and down the table sides.

Attempting to determine how this embarrassment came about, she searched her memory. The raucous noise, swirling scents, and heated bodies of the earlier evening at the bar came back. Lilith had fended off several attempts by men to hook up. Most presented very clichéd or gross opening lines. One even waltzed up, placed a possessive elbow on the bar, and opened with a goofy look and a whisper, "I'd like to watch you eat a banana."

She had smiled and responded, "Find me a banana."

A look of hope infused the man-boy's face. She grabbed his throat in a one-handed chokehold, pulled him close, and completed her thought, "So I can stuff it up your ass."

Five minutes later, a pleasant tenor voice said. "Boy, what a jerk. He lost the bet his drinking buddies proposed."

Lilith turned and spotted a blond-haired Germanic-featured man, his assurance, and slight widow's peak, suggesting an age in the late thirties. "What bet?"

"I was sitting next to their table. You were selected as the mark of the evening – could he get you in bed." He offered a hand. "Such a pleasure to see you work him over."

The handshake was firm and dry. Lilith made room for him at the bar. She noted gray Gucci slacks and a long-sleeved pink Polo shirt. The watch a Rolex Submariner — perhaps, he liked diving — shoes, black buffalo-leather loafers. The fragrance of his body wash came across as crushed cherry and fresh cut wood.

"I'm Ron Jones." He waved the bartender over. "What are you drinking?"

"I'll have a Moscow Mule." Lilith continued her examination. Impeccable haircut, and nails recently manicured. She sniffed — his cologne Armani Code Sport — and underneath a slight tinge of blood. She looked for a shaving cut.

Cocking her head, Lilith raised an eyebrow, and said, "So what is your shtick?"

He replied, "Investment banker, Citi Bank." He turned his back, momentarily hiding their drinks, while he paid the bartender.

The cocktail was strong; the heavy ginger flavor did not hide the fact that it was a double.

Ron must have some informal agreement with the bartender.

Well, she thought, he would drop well before she did. She had out drunk some of the world's mightiest tipplers over the centuries. Many had tried the old *candy is dandy, but liquor is quicker* formula to their disappointment. If Lilith required an energy jolt, suitors did not need any sweet words or artificial inducement. If she were fully charged, no force or ploy would work.

Ron started talking about their leaving together after the first drink. He seemed surprised when Lilith refused. He ordered a second round. They talked about the New York Music scene and discussed the Met's latest opera, Verdi's *Aida.* Lilith's favorite, a performance of *Carmen,* was opening next week.

She remembered using that name during her workdays at the Seville *Real Fábrica de Tabacos,* the Spanish Kings' Royal Tobacco Factory in the early 1800s. Part of the wild band of women cigar workers, whose jobs bought them enough financial independence to not need a husband. She and they lived scandalously, picking their lovers. Their stories ended up in a novella by Prosper Mérimée, which was used by Bizet for the basis of his opera *Carmen.*

During her last visit to Seville, a year ago, she noticed the old stomping ground had been turned into a university. Well, she and her sisters had matriculated from that hard school. Lilith felt glad others were getting their chance from a more gentile institution.

A voice from behind brought her back into the decaying old house and her present dilemma. "Well, you certainly drank enough Flunitrazepam to put an elephant to sleep. Three doubles with Rohypnol seeded in each. Didn't think you'd ever go under."

Lilith decided to play it innocent. "Where are we? Why..."

"Yes, I even had your banana boyfriend help haul you out to the car. Just another drunken woman being helped home by a friend. Remember, *'Friends don't let friends drive drunk.'* "

Lilith turned her head to the left, the wire bit into her neck. Another head lolled over an adjacent table. The man apparently worked two victims at a time. The face lay too much in the shadow to tell if it was their clients' daughter. She put a quiver in her voice, "Please let me go. We can have fun without all this."

"Sorry, I can't get it up without staging things properly. Nasty childhood and all that. Now, let's see how well you can scream."

Lilith decided to oblige him. She could break windows if necessary.

She heard metal objects clink together in the background. The man's breathing deepened. A fiery slicing pain started at her neck and ran quickly down her spine. She gasped, damped the sting, and gave him the scream he wanted.

Using a variety of scalpels and knives, he carved quarter-inch deep cuts in vine patterns on the skin of her back and buttocks. Blood flowed freely to drip off her sides, shoulders, and bottom, trapped by the plastic. Lilith mentally reduced her sensitivity to pain, but kept up a babble of pleas, curses, and moans.

Her mind supplied other times of torment. She remembered being tortured by the Crusaders during the sack of Jerusalem in 1099, by the Mongols in 1258 after the fall of Baghdad, and by numerous others before and after. This guy was a gross, incompetent amateur by comparison.

Five minutes later, he gasped, "That's it, that is it!"

His current cutting blade fell to the floor. He smacked up against her, his male member entered her dog style.

Lilith gave him another convincing scream. The rape was just what she needed. *'Please, Brer Fox, please don't throw me into the briar patch,'* she thought.

She could feel he wore a condom so as not to leave any DNA trace. That was no good, the latex being an insulator would weaken the energy transfer. Lilith worked the muscles surrounding her vagina. There were many more multidirectional layers than normal women possessed and thousands of years' experience using them. At about the third stroke, the protection was squeezed off. Well into the male animal-focus, he did not notice. She applied the muscles in the exquisite ways she had practiced over the centuries. The killer's groans turned into ululations, the energy blowing out of him.

The man over-balanced, staggered, bumped against his tool bench. Knives and other metallic instruments clattered to the floor. She heard him fall into a chair – a rocker, its runners squeaked three times. Silence filled the room, only interrupted by heavy breathing. Lilith used the new power charge to coagulate the blood dribbling from her cuts. Energized muscle and skin cells rapidly reproduced. The cuts began to seal.

She strained against her bonds. To spite her demonic strength, the duct tape and the wire resisted successfully. For the next four hours, she listened to noises originating outside. Several times a train went by, close enough to feel the vibration from steel wheels on the steel track. She counted those passing, one dashed by quickly, probably a commuter train. Car lights flashed through the ragged curtains of a dirty bay window and flitted across the far wall. Gravel popped from beneath tires. She relaxed. Struggling only tightened the bonds, if she could only get the taped wrists to her teeth.

The serial man, Ron, probably not his real name, moaned. The rocker creaked. "Shit, what happened? Fell asleep." He looked at his Rolex, "Damn, its late. I've got to hurry."

*

The serial killer pulled Lilith, wrapped in plastic to the neck, from the trunk of his car, and let her thump to the ground. A false dawn, combined with her superior night vision, provided enough light to see his license plate. The smell of cut sod and freshly shoveled dirt came to her nostrils, along with the nitrous oxide diesel smell of the car exhaust.

Still weak, the man pulled out the second victim and did a wobbly fireman's carry to a shallow grave. Tossed from his shoulders, the body smacked into the trench bottom with all the grace and heft of a solid-rubber manikin. Lilith watched the killer's silhouette as he scooped dirt back into the grave, and then placed thc original sod over the fresh soil. She figured it would be a day or two before he fully recovered from her taking from his life force. Gasping for air, he paused to allow his stressed heart to slow.

The plastic sheath had loosened during the ride. She managed to get her hands up to her chin. The strength to lift her gone, Ron grabbed a fistful of sheeting at her ankles and began dragging her to the second hole. He kneeled twice, to rest and catch his breath. Drops of sweat splatted onto her plastic shroud. At the graveside, he twisted her ankles to slip her into the hole facedown.

A bag of wadded clothes and personal effects dropped on her feet. The sunrise reflected off his stainless-steel watch as he shoveled and pushed dirt over her body and head.

Lilith waited until she heard the car noise fade out. The man had been too weak to dig deep. She was maybe three feet down. In the loose soil, she raised her wrists to her mouth and began to chew. The muscles in her neck and jaws pumped up. As in all other ways, her bite was much stronger, teeth much sharper, than humans could produce.

Shadows of trees across the field retreated as the sun rose higher. A coyote following the breeze stopped and snuffled at the edge of the woods. The smell of blood and fresh meat made it salivate. After completing a stiff-legged shuffle across the meadow, the scavenger began digging at the closest site. The canine cousin jerked, stopped, and cocked its head.

Its nose, ears, and instinct told the animal something was wrong. An arm shot up out of the soil, grabbing the scavenger by the throat. In terror, it squirmed and backpedaled.

A red-brown clay-stained head, with mud-plastered tresses, exploded up out of the ground. Teeth fastened on the coyote's neck. With a yank of her head, the resurrected Lilith tore off a massive chunk of fur and skin. A second neck-bite ripped open the animal's main artery.

🖋

Joe's face reflected the concern in his voice. "Well boy, where have you been? Lilith was missing and you were nowhere to be found. I was frantic."

Joe and Keean sat on brown leather Barcelona chairs in the detective agency's office.

Keean stiffened. He resented being called a boy, especially by someone infinitely younger. The last several days a blank while his sister controlled their shared body, he responded, "Just out experiencing the wonders of the city."

"You'll be glad to know your sister has had a narrow escape while on company business. I sent her to shower and bed an hour ago after her debrief." He waved a sheaf of papers.

Keean faked a look of anxiety on his face and started to get up. "Leave her alone. She needs sleep. Sit back down. I'll fill you in."

Joe walked to his worktable against the office's back wall and opened a cabinet. "You want coffee or booze?"

Keean scrunched in his chair, stretched arms, and then hugged himself. "Both."

Joe returned using a book as a tray with coffee cups and shot glasses. His companion knocked back the liquor. "Whoa, that's my good Balvenie single malt. You sip that stuff."

Keean shook his head and took up the coffee mug. "My back itches. It is killing me."

"Lilith told me you'd be affected, you being twins. Whatever affects one the other feels, both emotionally and physically. She says your bond is much stronger than most, even down to experiencing stigmata. Read about that once. *The Corsican Brothers*, right? Lift up your shirt."

Keean had suspected as much. Still, it was better Joe didn't know the truth. Humans' fear of demons ruined any possibility of a reasonable relationship. Prey didn't appreciate the predator. Irritated that Lilith hadn't told him herself, he ripped at his shirt; a button sailed off to rattle across the cherry wood floor. Joe opened a fist-sized can of ointment. "Lilith left this for you. Damn man, your back is crisscrossed with the same pattern of lines that maniac cut into your sister." He applied the paste. Keean jumped.

"Alright, relax. It's a combination of a topical anesthetic and an antibiotic. I'll tell you the story while I rub this stuff in."

"Your sister went to a target bar seeking to identify a serial killer, in the hopes of recovering the daughter of our latest clients. The mission was way too successful. The psychopath drugged her and hauled her off to carve and rape her. Just before daybreak, he moved her and the body of a previous victim to a private burial ground. After he left, Lilith managed to chew loose her bonds and dig her way out. She hitchhiked back, arriving about nine this morning. The good news: our clients' daughter was not among the victims of the killer. Chasing a different lead, I followed the trail of their pool boy. He bought two tickets to Miami the day of the daughter's disappearance and booked a room for two at the Shepley Hotel on the beach. Can you guess where the little darling and her credit cards are?"

His concern for his sister, and a rising sense of danger made Keean wish for more scotch. Serious trouble ahead, he thought, if Lilith had to relate her story to the police and possibly testify at a trial. They would be exposed. Men in black suits and clerical collars would descend on them en masse, and that would be no pun.

"Joe, we cannot let Lilith get in the middle of this. I know we want to put this nasty in the *caveola*..." Keean used a word from their time in ancient Rome. He shook his head, "I mean slammer. But our contract with you guarantees privacy."

"Easy, sit back and let me finish with the ointment and the story. I wish I knew what you two are so afraid of. Your sister covered her tracks and still left us with some information for the police."

"According to Lilith, her blood trace was captured by the plastic she was wrapped in. That sheeting is downstairs on the workbench waiting for incineration. A dead coyote carcass is buried in her place, which should contaminate most remaining signs of her.

"She got the license plate of the psychopath's car, which was diesel-fueled. A used condom is positioned in the grave of the other girl, so his DNA will be available for analysis. She drew a sketch of his face. We know the location of the burying ground and have narrowed the location of the torture house. The closest juncture of railroad and a gravel road gives us a choice of three houses. We've verified his pattern and can meet the fellow again at bar number twenty- five this coming Wednesday. The only question remaining is whether we want the police to take him or we do a citizen's arrest."

Keean's face flushed with anger. The killer would pay. His throat tightened. Working with the police on this could be tricky.

There was still the question of blood and skin trace left on the man's knives. And, surely, he would recognize Lilith, if they ever bumped into each other again. Even with the information they could give the police, there was no direct evidence, no actual witness that could testify in a trial. The man might get off.

Worry made his stomach muscles twitch. The serial killer tried to relax into his Ron Jones, Investment Banker persona. Stopping outside the bar entrance, he popped an antacid. These last seven days had been spent listening to police radio and watching the news for any sign that someone had spotted his hurried disposal of the last two honeys. A crooked smile appeared as he thought about the great harem that he had possessed.

Besides pleasing his mind and body, disposal of their assets elevated his lifestyle. He kept any cash, used ATM cards to drain their accounts, and sold credit cards, and sometimes cars through the black markets rife throughout the city.

In that regard, the one from last week had been disappointing. Little cash, no cards, and not even an ID carried. The sex, however, preternaturally good, an experience that had exhilarated him from hair follicles to toe nails. It had taken him a good forty-eight hours to recover. He should have kept her around for a while.

A pair of girls ahead of him giggled as they waited in line, reminding him what he was here for. A jocular feeling blossomed in his mind, the muscles in his face and neck relaxed, he assured himself that the hunting would be good tonight.

The queue moved forward. He passed the door attendant's inspection and entered. The atmosphere of the bar wrapped around him. Air conditioners struggled with heat generated by flashing laser lights and the writhing bodies of dancers. Off in one corner the sound of clacking pool balls meshed with groans and cries of delight as striped or solid colored balls dropped into or missed pockets. The background level of conversation grew in amplitude as voices raised to compete with the music and themselves. A regular hive hum, he thought.

The smell of it, rum, scotch, and gin mixed with sweat and the fugue of a hundred artificial scents. The colognes, deodorants, lotions, and hair sprays, all blended into a swirling, exciting, fragrant overkill. He dodged away from a server with an overloaded tray of iced drinks headed for the tables behind him, an invisible prow before her parting the crowd.

Drawing the Ron persona to the surface, he began to examine the night's batch of women. Those too girlish in dress or behavior rejected, he preferred the more mature of personality and body. Those resembling his mother and sisters were more to his taste. He followed one dark-haired, curvaceous specimen to the bar. After introducing himself, she accepted his offer.

15

Waving the bartender over, he read the man's nametag, ordered drinks, and whispered, "Bill, make the lady's doubles, mine singles." Popping a folded Grant into the man's hand, he received a wink in return. The barman returned to the drink station to fill the order. Ron checked his pocket for the drug bottle.

Looking left, he noticed a new arrival in discussion with Bill, as his hands mixed the drinks. The stranger's profile looked familiar. Black clothes — shoes, slacks, sport coat, and long collared shirt, all black — matched the fellow's hair. The man unfolded a pencil sketch, handed it to Bill. After wiping hands on a towel, the barman held the sketch up to the light. Eyebrows twitched, lips pressed together, Bill started a negative shake of his head. He paused and took a closer look.

Instinctively, the bartender looked down the bar. The man in black's head followed. As their eyes met, Ron felt a frisson turn his spine into ice. The face resembled the woman from last week! The man grabbed the sketch and leaped off the barstool.

Survival instinct kicked in. Ron spun and plunged into the writhing mob. He plowed between two dancing couples, swatting them aside with outstretched arms. He changed tactics and began dodging left and right around undulating pairs. Reaching a back wall, he lunged left past the restrooms towards the red-lit exit sign. He hit the crash bar. The door resisted, then swung open, leaving him to stagger into an alley.

16

Not stopping to look behind, Ron ran full speed, reached the street, and turned left. Behind him, he heard the alley door slam open. A dark figure took position behind him. The entrances of stores and boutiques closed for the night blurred in his side vision. The sound of running feet scratching the cement came from behind.

A lighted store window caught his attention. Skidding to a halt, he entered an all-night Korean market, slammed the door, and clicked the deadlock. A heavy body crashed against the frame. The store windows vibrated.

Ron ran. Shouts in Korean and English followed him. The glass in the front door shattered. He ran out the back into another alley. Racing out to the street, he spotted a cab letting out a fare. Leaping into the vehicle's backseat, he shouted, "Let's go! Let's go!"

Confused by his fright, the cabby responded, "Where?"

The window next to Ron shattered. A long arm punched in, a fist-full of brass knuckles grazed his nose. The cabby caught the panic and floored the accelerator. Out the back window, Ron saw the man in black grow smaller. The thick metal rings enclosing his fist gave out a bronze glint in the streetlight.

Time now to answer the cabby's question. "Take me to the closest car rental office." He'd have to pick up his Mercedes later, no way he was returning to the vicinity of that bar this evening.

17

The old torture house looked dark and bleak. It would be his sanctuary tonight. The yellow Chevy Cruise rental car swayed on its suspension as it rocked in and out of the driveway chuckholes. He parked to one side, between pine trees and overgrown azaleas, where it could not be seen from the county access road. Ron pushed the driver's door open against resisting bushes. Their budding, half-leafed limbs swatted against his pant legs. Scrapping the mud off his shoes against the concrete steps, he unlocked and opened the front door of the hideaway.

The deadlock was a special variety; it used the same key both inside and outside to throw or retract the bolt. There was no inside locking knob to turn. A grim smile twisted his lips. He was a detail man. If one of his honeys managed to get out of her bonds, she still couldn't unlock the door. That and the grates installed over the windows kept his captives nice and secure, even if loose inside.

Ron locked the door and turned. The lights flashed on. He jumped. A female voice came from the back, "I thought you would never get here."

A shock wave racked his body. Walking towards him was the woman from last week. Dressed in black slacks, shirt, and sports coat, she presented an exact match of the man chasing him. The floor creaked as she advanced. A thin-lipped smile and dark-slitted eyes pinned him, like a bug under a magnifying glass.

"No! I buried you."

"A wider smile came that bared canine-looking teeth, "So you did."

A shudder ran through his body. Hands shook. Keys dropped. He turned and jerked the door. It refused to open. He spun around and swung an arm, fist closed.

The woman pulled his arm towards her, turned to allow his forward motion to land him on her back, pumped her legs, and tossed him over her head. Ron landed with a crash. Dazed, he watched her drop on his chest. Breath belched out. Driven by muscle and a bodyweight much heavier than possible, the open palm of her hand drove up under his chin. His last memory was of front teeth breaking.

*

Ron woke. Covered with goosebumps, his jaw and teeth ached. He felt funny. His body light like gravity had been suspended. A slap to a cheek popped his eyes open. Before him, stood 'the woman.'

"You do *not* look that good naked," she said.

Ron tried to move. His body jiggled. He was suspended vertically in some kind of frame, arms and legs splayed out, both front and backside exposed. He moaned and tried to free his appendages. No luck, they were duct-taped, his own tape used, to the rig. He looked around.

They were in some kind of box, the walls, floor, and ceiling all plastic sheeting.

Ron examined his captor. She had dressed for the work. A plastic poncho covered the majority of her body. Her hair was bound up in a scarf of the same material, hands covered with double latex gloves, and bare feet encased in plastic covers bound at the ankle. The serial killer in him admired her preparations. The 360-degree curtains would completely contain blood splatter. No fluids or flesh would be found on her body, in her protected hair or under finger or toenails.

"Besides paying for your sins, I thought you would appreciate a lesson from a professional. You really are an amateur at torture."

"How did you find me?"

"Well, I'd been here before, remember? We deduced your pattern. It was a simple case to have my brother track you."

"That man trying to catch me, your brother?"

"Yes. But it was never our plan to grab you in the city. What could we have done there with all those potential witnesses? He was just a beater in the hunt. Just a distraction to drive you to your hidey-hole and the real trap."

Ron noticed his workbench had been moved inside the plastic room. Besides his tools, there were sandwiches, a half-dozen Twinkies, bottles of Perrier water, a tank labeled oxy-propane with tubing attached, and, remarkably, one of those Bingo rotating wire baskets with the side handle. His heart began to pound.

Lilith caught his glance. "While you were demonstrating your incompetence last week, I remembered what the Mongols did to the princes of Baghdad. Something they borrowed from the Chinese. It is called *lingchi,* literally, ascending a mountain slowly. It was used for only the most severe crimes." She waved towards the food. "I have laid in supplies, since this may take a very long time."

A shiver ran through Ron's skin. He convulsed his limbs and bucked his body. The confining rig, attached up and down, rafter to floor, with chains, absorbed his energy.

"The Bingo thingy is a refinement of my own. There are seventy-five balls with alphanumeric codes. I spin the cage, and a random ball drops out. I consult a chart that tells me which body part needs attention. Once we have used all the balls, I refill the cage and we start over."

"No, I have money! A lot! I can pay you."

Lilith picked out a Bingo ball labeled B5. She consulted the chart and picked up a scalpel with a two-inch blade. "Not to worry, you will tell me everything you know and give me everything you have well before this ends."

21

Her left hand came up to tickle his right nipple. It grew hard. She pinioned the nipple tip between blade and thumb. He gasped for breath.

"Now, how many women have you killed?"

"Nooooo! No! I couldn't help it. There's a demon in me. I promise never to do it again." Without volition, his hands and feet flapped.

"No, I know demons. Not one in you, just poor, warped psychopathic humanity." Her eyebrows wiggled, "But there is a real demon here tonight."

Her fingers twitched, a half-inch of nipple detached. Ron gasped and bit his lips. Blood dripped down his ribs.

In a fake voice of kindness, Lilith said, "Now, we do not want you to bleed out, do we?"

Placing the scalpel on the bench, she picked up the oxy-propane tank with its trailing hose and brass nozzle. She spoke, as fingers adjusted the regulator, "In case you are not aware, this is a jeweler's torch. It can melt silver and gold. Tonight, we use it to cauterize. You will last a lot longer this way."

The torch spurted a thin blue flame. Ron felt his mouth drop open. She applied the nozzle. From his diaphragm came a scream. A burnt pork smell assaulted his nostrils.

Lilith spun the cage, consulted a second Bingo ball, and then the chart. "Aha. My favorite."

He watched her reach between his legs. Ron felt her pull his scrotum out. He jerked and moaned as a long knife cut a slit in the lower part. Latex-gloved fingers reached inside, extracted his testicles. An expert slash and the bloody brace lay in her palm.

She tossed them into a black plastic thirty-gallon drum and reached for the torch. Ron bawled. He heard his own high-pitched castrati squeal follow a moment later.

A Night at the Bronx Zoo

Lilith spotted something in their peripheral vision. She spoke inside Keean's head.

"Something approaches. Be alert."

The tall grass rippled, then stopped. A delta-shaped head on what appeared to be a flexible hose of some kind peered above the undergrowth.

"A snake. A boa or python."

The grass rippled again. The what-ever-it-was moved ten feet closer. "That's not the way a snake moves. It's more cat-like stalking – movement, then pausing so as not to alert the prey."

"Whatever it is, let's get the hell out of here. Leave the woman."

The scent Keean picked up was alien, mixed ungulate, reptilian, and lynx. The creature grew closer, if it was a cat, it was now within charging distance. No time to put on clothes, He stooped and backed slowly for the trees. A coughing roar disrupted the quiet. Keean turned and ran. Something long and sinewy leaped out of the brush.

Keean glanced over his shoulder. Bathed in the last of the twilight stood a beast he and his sister had never met, only heard about in stories.

Lilith chimed in. *"It's a chimera! Body of a lioness, head of a goat coming out of its right shoulder and an eight-foot-long snake in place of a tail."*

"Oh, is that all? And I thought we were in real trouble."

Another roar. *"Keep running asshole. Did I forget to mention, the snake can spit acid?"*

Keean increased his speed. He could hear and feel the thump of the animal's feet as it raced after them. "This just keeps getting better and better. Where did it come from? Why us?"

The creature was faster than him. He dodged off the trail into a grove of trees. The creature skittered past, reversed direction, and came after. Keean could feel its hot breath on his bare buttocks.

"Nothing like being naked to make one feel vulnerable."

"Shut up!" Keean gasped.

Ahead two redbud trees had grown together at the base forming a 'V' shape. Heart pounding, he bent at the knees, extended one leg, and hurtled through the open area. Too close to dodge around the chimera followed. Its four-hundred-pound body became stuck halfway through. It roared, bleated, and hissed. The trees shook. Tiny wine-colored flowers showered down.

Keean took advantage of the moment. "Why are you after us?"

The creature stopped writhing; six eyes focused. All three mouths opened; the coordinated combination of sounds mimicked human speech. "Kill you."

"Why? We have done nothing to you."

"Priests promise food, protection, mates." The snakehead catapulted forward and spit. Lilith shrilled, *"Let's go. Let's go. He's working himself free."*

Keean ran out of the copse, down the path, and across a mushy grass lawn where an automatic clock had turned on a sprinkler system.

"Good thinking. The water will wash away our scent. It will take the lion part a while to catch our smell again. The wind is out of the north. Go to the Goldman stone mill and take the bridge over the Bronx River. Traveling south will keep us downwind. The chimera will need to slow down periodically to smell out our footprints."

A few minutes later, Keean ran along the riverbank and turned right to cross the bridge. "How can we fight this thing?"

"Poorly. The chimera's outer skin is metallic. It can thicken it at will. Spears, arrows, bullets – no effect. Maybe a fifty-caliber browning could discourage it. Besides, we only have two arms to deal with what will be a three-prong attack. We need to lose it."

Keean heard the pad of heavy paws on the path behind him. He increased speed, found himself at the closed gates of the adjoining Bronx zoo, leaped up, clasped the top, and swung over. Behind him, a crash and a squeal of metal followed as the chimera broke through. It was dark inside the menagerie grounds; only a few security lights glimmered here and there.

He charged past the sea lions, the Madagascar exhibit, and the Komodo dragon enclosure. The creature caught up with them just beyond the zoo store. The Keean body turned to face their pursuer. The horns of the goat head butted him mid-section. He flew up into the air and smashed through the glass hood of a popcorn machine cart. Popped kernels flew up in a cloud, resembling an explosion of disturbed white moths.

Keean slid across the paved area and crashed to a stop up against a trash barrel, his body crushing it beyond repair. He pulled out its plastic bag liner. The cat portion of the creature caught him in its claws. The snakehead pitched forward. Keean pulled the trash can liner over its scaled head. The snake spit. The plastic caught the discharge. It melted. The hot semi-liquid synthetic wrap cooled and then glued itself to the snakehead. The writhing reptile head was now blind, its nostrils sealed, and its mouth clogged.

While his antagonist rolled on the ground in reaction, Keean slipped out of the lion portion's grasp. Dripping blood, he limped down the path and hid inside the kiddy bug carousel. It was like a regular merry-go-round, except instead of quadrupeds it substituted saddled insects: dragonflies, caterpillars, praying mantises, and such. Keean wedged himself in the shadows behind a fiberglass beetle.

"Oh, shit, a dung beetle! Couldn't you choose a better place." Lilith's voice changed. *"Damage report: Left kidney in shock, one rib broken, two cracked, lower portion of the liver injured, bruises and bleeding claw marks over right rib cage and on thighs. We've put one head out of business. However, it will adapt –"*

A crash and a tinkle. The carousel lit up and began to turn. Music played. The chimera had smacked into the power box. Keean had no choice. Their hideout exposed, he leaped out and ran past the Mouse House and 4-D Theater. He could hear the close-together scratch of claws on the hardtop of the path.

Coming to a 'T' he kept going straight leaping over bamboo fencing, concrete retaining wall, and moat into the African Plains exhibits. The wild dogs started howling. Monkeys screamed and shook tree branches. The giraffes were out in the moonlight. He ran under the legs of a big male. The chimera tried to follow and succeeded in bringing the twenty-foot tall, three-thousand-pound animal down on itself.

The delay in getting itself untangled gave Keean the time to scale several more walls and trenches, before landing in the lions' enclosure. The startled animals refused to close with him.

He soared over their moat and wall back onto a path in time to avoid the ensuing fight between a couple of males and the chimera. It didn't last long enough. The five personalities came together again outside the bear pits.

*

Big Ed, the Grizzly bear, was pissed. He lay on a cold stone floor in temporary quarters while being prepared to have surgery. An impacted molar sent agony stabbing through his jaw, driving him crazy. The pain medication had worn off an hour ago. His empty belly rumbled; the doctors had him on a water-only diet so he wouldn't throw up during the operation. On top of everything else, the two female brown bears next door were in heat and their scent had him aroused. Red insane rage hovered in the back of his skull. He rose and paced back and forth along the outside wall of his enclosure, unable to sleep. It seemed like the whole zoo was in an uproar. Monkeys screamed, birds squawked, and big cats roared. Whatever was stirring them up appeared to be coming his way. He sat back on his portly thighs and let out a slobbering bellow of his own.

*

Keean turned to face the closing chimera. It charged. He grabbed a goat horn, poked two spread fingers into the eyes of the lion, and hung on. Fortunately, the snake remained out of action, its plastic sheath confining it.

The energy of the chimera's charge carried the two locked together antagonists up and over the wall into Big Ed's pit. They landed with the chimera on top. Keean had the air knocked out of him. His spine made a crackling sound.

A moment of confusion in the bear's mind was instantly replaced by an explosion of fury. This intrusion was the last straw. The grizzly galloped forward and swung a paw. A loud crack. A chunk of curved goat horn went sailing off to splash in the bathing pool.

The chimera released Keean and turned to face the larger threat. The bear waded in with teeth and six-inch claws. Thin strips of metallic skin peeled off the chimera's back. Big Ed managed to bite off an ear before the lion portion doubled up and raked the bear's underbelly with its talons. Chunks of fur and skin flew. They jumped apart.

Keean gasped for air and watched the two circle each other. The bear was over twice the weight of its challenger. In its berserker madness, it wouldn't know when to quit. The grizzly leaped forward and clawed the right rear flank of the chimera. The chimera caught the offending paw in its mouth and bit off a toe. Big Ed seemed impervious to pain. He picked up the intruder and tossed it into the pond. Struggling to its feet, the doused chimera realized the match was too unequal. Two of its heads were out of action, and the bear was fresh, twice as big, and fast. The monster bounded out of the water. Chased by Big Ed, it ran up the outstretched trunk of the old dead tree kept in the pit as a scratching post and soared out of the pit.

Keean crawled up a sidewall and dropped into the adjacent female bear pit. The pair of sows kept their distance as he climbed up their barrier and onto the observation path. Bones ached, and wounds itched. Now, to find something to wear and to get home. He figured he could break into the zoo store for a t-shirt, hat, and shorts.

"This is like a bad reoccurring dream – the second time in six months you've left us naked in public, dickwad."

Freudian Slips

It's 1939 and only a few weeks away from the beginning of World War II. Passengers aboard the luxury cruise ship Normandie on its last voyage to New York, Keean and Lilith try to avoid the snares of three countries' intelligence services. Besides being brother and sister, Lilith and Keean Kleinfelt are a succubus/incubus—two demons, one male, one female cursed for eternity to inhabit one body. They morph back and forth between male and female aspects as needed for their seductions and the stealing of money and life force from their victims. The pair is over 350,000 years old and carry the burden of countless historical moments. Keean relives an old memory while at breakfast in the ship's lounge.

I remember 1889. Lilith and I were between swindles. We frequented Café Central, a popular Austrian *Kaffeehäuse*, where we planned our seductions and scams. The Baroque Vienna coffee house on the corner of Herrengasse and Strauchgasse had been around a while and counted among its past patrons Beethoven and Goethe. It was there I met Sigmund Freud, a man seeking a mission.

My sister, currently subordinate, our bodies and minds meshed together, speaks inside our intertwined brains. Her comments unheard by outsiders.

Keean, let's have a Fiaker. Double schlag and two cherries on top.

The sugared espresso is mixed with Kirschwasser, a dry cherry brandy, and topped with two dollops of whipped cream. I shake my head.

I whisper, "Lilith it's too sweet."

We have a big day and night ahead of us. I want some luxury while we have a peaceful moment to enjoy it. Besides, there is a masked ball this evening and I am thinking about our costume. I want to attract only the most vigorous prey tonight.

I refuse and she quiets into a sulk. The atmosphere of the place is peaceful enough. Dark wood paneling and furniture absorbs the light coming in from half-windows and gaslight fixtures, leaving a dim and somber atmosphere. Marble Corinthian columns hold up a vaulted ceiling. A heavy gulp of air rewards the breather with the lung-sting of concentrated cigar and cigarette smoke.

Sipping a *grosser Schwarzer,* a double shot of espresso, I read the morning edition of the *Deutsche Zeitung.* My stomach tells me it is time for lunch and my mind wavers between schnitzel or a bowl of goulash soup.

I hear the piano render some passages from *Mozart's Die Zauberflote.* Gustaf Mahler, the director of the Vienna Court Opera fingers the keys between sips of coffee and bites of apricot dumplings. He licks off the powdered sugar after each bite.

A mustachioed waiter passes, his face set in a frown. They always have trouble getting the keys cleaned after Mahler's use. I hear chair legs rasp and their joints squeak as a person sits across from me.

"Herr Kleinfelt, I hope you don't mind my intrusion."

Dropping the newspaper, I am confronted by a dark-haired man with a neatly trimmed beard. I tilt my head, lean forward, and give him a wolf smile. This is usually enough to discourage an unwanted contact. His eyebrows rise.

"I understand your desire to be alone. Immortals must frequently tire of their immersion in humanity."

Lilith awakes from wherever she was drifting. *Keean, quiz this man. If he is a danger, we may need to leave Vienna or kill him.*

I cover my shock by placing my elbows on the table and cup my chin in my hands. "You need to tell me who you are and why you insult me with such nonsense."

"Gladly. I am Herr Doktor Sigmund Freud and I hope to break new ground in the treatment of ailments hidden in the mind. I present no threat to you and seek to learn from your experience, which must be vast."

34

I drop my hands to the table and finger the butter knife used earlier on my breakfast roll.

The man sees my action and moves back in his chair.

Calm down, brother, we cannot take him out here, too many witnesses. We can decide what to do later. In the meantime, do a question for a question.

I relax and let the knife slip back onto the linen tablecloth. A sip of my espresso tells me it needs replacement. "Herr Doktor Freud, I was about to have lunch would you join me?"

"The whole afternoon is open for me."

We give our order to the waiter, and I begin the dialogue. "What makes you think I am immortal?"

The man pauses to light up a cigar. After a few puffs, he says, "It started with three of my female patients. They all experienced the same symptoms: melancholia, lack of appetite, and physical weakness, as if their vitality had been drained. Their only commonality, relationships with you."

"This is an age of illness, both great and small sicknesses. Are you saying I am infecting my acquaintances?"

"The connection merely pointed me in your direction. As the Bible says, 'seek and ye shall find.' I have been watching you for the last three months. In addition, at my request, your movements have been backtracked in government records. My associates and friends in places you have lived have verified your long ago past in interviews, some with very old people.

Even earlier imprints of your activities were found in newspapers, travel documents, and personal diaries that came into their possession. We stopped the research after going back three hundred years."

"Even if I was as old as Methuselah — " *or, even older,* — "that does not qualify me to cure their bodies."

"Don't try to tangle us in irrelevances, *Mein Herr*. Many times, physical indications are merely symptoms." Freud taps his forehead. "The root causes are here. There I have gone and discovered your victims' maladies are short-lived. Three days to a week, and they are back to normal."

Keean, this man is exceptionally perceptive. Lilith giggles in my mind. *Deliciously so. Finally, a human male who can present a challenge.*

I also point at his head. "And, my friend, what process do you use to understand what goes on in there."

"Two years ago, I coined a term for it: psychoanalysis."

"So, like so many, you turn to the Greeks. *Psykhe,* the butterfly-winged goddess of the soul, might not like you using her name. But combining soul with analysis, this second word's original meaning to break up or loosen, does create an interesting combination word – breaking up or loosening the soul."

"The word is just the beginning. I have a theory, and it needs someone like you to test it against."

I begin laughing and can't stop. Cramming my napkin in my mouth, muffles the explosion. Lilith joins in, her feminine shriek rising in my head to the edge of hysteria. I choke but cough out the words.

"You can't analyze us... me, I do not have a soul."

Freud blushes. He takes a long draw on his cigar. "I don't wish to analyze you. Don't care if you are an angel, god, or demon. I just want your comments on my theory. You must have more insight into human behavior than any other living being."

Lilith gives a final chuckle. *Let's pursue this, brother. It may help us find ways to take our human prey more easily. Besides, if we anger him, he may turn his findings about us over to the authorities. Witch burnings are recent past here.*

"All right," I respond, "how do you discover things hidden behind skin and skull? And, separate the truths from the lies that emerge."

"That is one of the problems. My friend, Josef Breuer, has used hypnosis. The technique allowed a hysterical female patient complaining of bizarre symptoms, such as headaches, blurred vision, legs or arms temporarily paralyzed, and horrifying visions to tell him what was oppressing her mind.

"It seems she was terrified of her sick father's imminent death and the realization it brought of her own mortality. When she talked freely about her feelings, the symptoms would disappear. She called it the 'talking cure.'"

"So, how has that modus operandi worked for you?"

"Not so good. Some patients resist hypnosis; some cannot be hypnotized. Have you any suggestions?"

Lilith feeds me words, which I repeat. "Our... my experience is humans love to talk, even those that appear silent and bound up inside. Get them talking. At appropriate intervals, ask open-ended questions, sit back, and listen to them relate all their enigmas. One secret freely exposed will lead to multiple associations."

Of course, we use the information gathered to exploit our marks' weaknesses.

Freud's eyebrows shoot up; fingers wiggle like excited worms. "Ah! This method... this... this *free association* could be the entrance into the mind."

I cock my head to the left. "And what do you expect to find there?"

"I have come to believe that human behavior is heavily influenced by instinct. What have you discovered?"

The waiter brings plates of *Kaiserschmarren,* slices of cake, and new cups, the facedown coffee spoon on their tops a sign of being freshly filled up, a mark of Hapsburg politeness.

Lilith pauses until the waiter leaves, and then instructs me to continue. "I would agree. Although it is difficult for me to opine on a capacity I do not possess. I was created with few discernable instincts, they being substitutes for rational decision-making. However, my observations dictate that the non-physical part of the mind comes in at least three parts. There is the part that talks and manages the human's daily actions and then there is a capacity for violence and greed offset, mostly, by another separate altruistic force."

Freud slams his palm on the table, rattling the glassware and spooking the nearby customers. "That makes sense! I perceive it. The two counteracting parts pushing and picking at the middle force...that fraction which declaims to the outside world what they are – the ego, the *I am*."

Now, brother, give him the good part. The overriding characteristic that makes our predation possible.

"Once you enter the mind, any human mind, any age, any gender, you will find a vast sexuality flooding every portion – expressing itself in different ways as humans age."

My dinner companion rocks back in his chair, chews on the butt end of his cigar. "You can't mean from birth on."

I pull my watch from a vest pocket and flip open the lid. "I certainly do, but there is not time now to go into it further. Let us gather in one week at this time and table, Herr Doktor."

Freud examines the remnants of his cigar with distaste, pulls another from an inside coat pocket and lights it. "I will be here, Herr Kleinfelt. You have given me much to pursue. *Auf Wiedersehn.*"

❦

The memory fades. Nodding to myself, I remember it wasn't *Auf Wiedersehn,* which means 'see you again soon,' but *lebewohl*, meaning 'farewell.' As a precaution, Lilith and I left that night, not returning to Europe until after WWI. By that time, Freud was too wrapped up defending his theories to wonder about us. He never spoke or wrote of our contribution to his theories.

Poems from *Near Death/Near Life*
Published by Prolific Press in 2015.

MY ASIAN SON LIFTS WEIGHTS

Black cast iron disks
ring together
with each of his curls,
a musical beat in 4/4 time.
On the TV, a PBS crew
explores the ancient
Ch'in emperor's tomb,

An army of terracotta soldiers
arranged there on parade.
The cameras do profiles,
pans and close-ups
of the statues thin-lipped faces,
high cheekbones and Asian eyes.

On the screen
my son's reflected image
animates the molded faces,
as if he had been the model

for the 2000-year-old sculpted clay.
The empty shells clutch life:
brows lift, black eyes shine again,
gray pottery cheeks flush to tan,
lips part and nostrils flare.

Finished with his sets,
a red Hibiscus silk shirt
pulled over his head,
my son strides from the house.
In his silvered sunglasses
shields flash, banners wave—
ten thousand warriors bow.

MEMORY OF A EURASIAN WORKING GIRL

I hope she knew why I was so quiet,
when we held hands at night in her strange land,
uninvited and lost.

It must have made her uneasy, watching for cues
from this twice her size round-eyed male creature,
so large pored and hairy.

Blood-warm breeze felt so comfortable.
Her perfume riffing the air,
set time for the music.

That evening she pierced my blind stare,
and helped me lay down my mountain of stored up death,
so weary with the weight.

Whether she was aware or not,
she did what women have done for soldiers
these thousands of futile years.

Fingers entwined, our primal spirits touched.
and I remembered
what my soul should look like.

Stories from *Free Fire Zone*

A book of seventeen short stories published in 2016 by Prolific
Press.

*Welcome to stories from the free fire zone. In Vietnam, it was
enemy territory. Anyone found there could be killed on sight, no
questions asked. Rod Teigler, the principal in the stories, comes from
a long line of American military men. As a result of government
experimentation and under the stress of life and death situations, he
suffers from multiple personality disorder. A reptilian berserk persona
straight from the amygdala grows stronger with every appearance.
The normal Rod and his wild counterpart must be reconciled, or the
body they both inhabit must die. In the book, each story is introduced
with a poem.*

MONSOON MALARIAL DREAMS 1967

*MEFLOQUINE (Lariam) – An antimalarial agent given soldiers
during the Vietnam War. Side effects included stomach upset,
dizziness, vivid (good, bad, erotic, and otherwise) dreams, insomnia
and anxiety. More serious side effects, such as seizures and psychosis,
were relatively rare.*

Locked within hip-swaying pillars of rain
long-nailed Asian temple dancers

weave hands in sly snake patterns.
Ankle bracelets shake, sunbreak-silver,
above toe-ringed bare feet.

Drops lash our helmets, enamel
the smooth steel surfaces, their striking
sacrificial voices a chorus-hum. Wind lips
press against our black rifle muzzles, create
muted atonal metal flutes.

Jungle mud amoebas grasp our calves,
murmur the seduction of Nirvana.
Without thought our muscles resist. Minds,
thorn-pierced by killing, seek nothingness.

We are shredded ripped leaves jinking
in the windborne water. Friend's faces
tatter, erode in the torrent. Stripped
to the seed, our souls' symmetry leaches away.

GROUP THERAPY

Beth wheeled her VW Jetta into the Veteran's Hospital parking lot and pulled into the section reserved for employees. Its elderly fender-rusted hulk clanked and shook for several minutes as two of the four cylinders kept firing even though the key was off. While she waited for the vehicle to finish its rumba, she read the sign positioned in the front center of her spot:

Reserved for Dr. Elizabeth Mueller, MD. Only a month into her tenure at the VA, the paint remained bright and shiny compared to the weathered boards of her co-workers. After all those years of education and internships, her first job had blossomed into something better than expected.

And now to actually have money, already the fruits of two paydays past gave some weight to her new bank account. Most of the first check had gone for apartment damage and utility deposits, as well as some basic furniture. The second went for clothes befitting her new profession. The third would provide part of the down payment for a new car, well... new-used car. No more bang-bang Jetta.

She walked the half block to her office, holding her skirt down at random intervals from the attentions of a frisky wind. Pastel orange and brown leaves swirled, many accumulated in awkward dead spots up against buildings and fences. Beth kicked a large jumble of lobed oak leaves away from the double doors of her building and entered. The old two-story Victorian-style red-brick pile had once been the residence of a long line of hospital administrators, beginning in the late 1800s. The hospital behind it had been rebuilt or expanded several times, as its patchwork of architectural styles testified—usually following major wars—when the demands of returning veterans forced the issue. Nowadays, the detached house soldiered on as the *Psychosocial Rehabilitation Recovery Center*. Pushing the doors closed until they clicked, she turned and carefully wiped her feet on the large gray-ribbed rug covering the entrance.

"That's a good girl," came from a scratchy voice. "Remember the all-staff meeting at four today."

"Good morning, Alma," Beth replied. "It's on my list. I've got four wives arriving in an hour. Send them up as they check in."

The receptionist nodded a fuzzy hennaed head and turned back to her keyboard. "Oh," Beth added, "does your granddaughter have any Girl Scout cookies left? Let me have two boxes of the peanut butter and one of the thin mints."

"I'll bring them in tomorrow."

Beth chalked up a score in her mental account book. Getting and staying on Alma's good side could only help a new person. A senior employee with thirty years in the VA, the aging receptionist knew everyone and everything, good and evil, about the hospital. Her network had tentacles in every nook and cranny. If so inclined, she could cover your ass, or expose it buck-naked. Besides, as a product of a fifties' secretarial school, she knew shorthand, a skill not taught anymore in this computer-rich age. The technique came in very handy on those occasions when the more keyboard challenged, such as herself, needed a speedy document.

Beth loved her office. The honey-colored oak floors creaked faintly with human steps; a bit loose after a century of wear.

Refinished a decade ago, they still looked good except for a warped spot caused by a window leak. The wooden desk dated back to WWII but had come around with some polish and scar wax. A modern ergonomic executive chair paired with the desk and a banker's lamp made an acceptable workstation. Lots of natural light flooded in through three floor-to-ceiling French windows to reflect off cream painted walls. A braided blue-green oval wool rug surrounded by a well-broken in couch and overstuffed chair completed the picture, the furniture's old dark leather exuded a classy scent.

Several ladder-backed chairs rested against the north wall's rail molding providing extra seating. Beth owned the framed Monet reproductions positioned on the walls, one of green-washed water Lilies and the other of an overflowing purple iris a garden. Her own bentwood rocker, a three-generation family heirloom, allowed her to come out from behind the desk and join clients for a more relaxed atmosphere—the informality especially needed today.

She would be conducting an initial group therapy session with four Vietnam veterans' wives. Although of varying ages, all had children. Beth selected some items from a blue enameled toy box in the corner. She carefully placed a Raggedy Ann doll with a frilly apron, several well-used Tonka trucks, and rainbow-colored Lego's centrally on the rug. Perhaps this new group would feel more relaxed, more talkative with these decorations, even though children would not be present today. They also helped calm her shaking hands. This would be her first wives' group.

"Get them settled, ask your questions, and don't talk, just listen," her mentor and boss Doctor Waszlowski had said. "They aren't here to get caught up on the latest psychobabble bullshit."

"What if they ask me to comment, or make a judgment?"

"Many questions will be rhetorical. They don't expect an answer. Just acknowledge the communication and pencil a note in your book. If they specifically want a response, ask them what they think. Or, if they are persistent, trust your instincts. If you don't feel comfortable answering say so."

A fluttery knock at the door scuttled her replay of yesterday's advisory session. At her invitation, three women entered, all with either coffee or tea—Alma's acts of kindness. They took seats, one at each end of the couch and the third in the overstuffed chair. Nervous eyes roamed over the office and took in Beth's features. They raised cups to their lips simultaneously, noted the fact and then laughed together.

"We're expecting one more person for our group," Beth announced, settling in the Bentwood. "How about that weather? Anyone blown off the road?"

A litany of complaints and wind-related stories followed, that expanded to fill the next five minutes. The conversation ended and the room quieted. Beth tried to think of something to say. Her sweat glands started stressing her deodorant. A tap on the door saved the day. Their fourth arrived.

"Sorry, a semi-truck overturned on the highway… down to one lane," a pixie cut redhead said, swooping down on one of the ladder-back chairs. She dropped a green faux-leather shoulder bag on the floor and extracted a bottle of Evian water.

"I hope we will all freely share our thoughts and concerns as we get to know each other," Beth announced. "Let's get started by giving our first names and telling us something about each other and our families. Who will start first?"

⌒

The session over, the mind-numbed psychiatrist eased back in her chair and slipped off her high heels. Alma entered, handed her a cut-crystal glass of cold orange juice, and departed. It felt like heaven going down a dry mouth and throat. Beth moved to the desktop keyboard and started typing notes. Let's see, she thought, first there's Elena: thin California-born Latina with a migrant picker's second-grade education, two middle school boys, and a husband who spent a tour in Nam as part of the Ninth Marines.

"Not an ex-marine," Elena said. "Once a marine always a marine, and that honey is the trouble."

At his worst when drinking, Humberto would rage and threaten his wife and kids. The family remained entirely dependent upon Elena's earnings from hotel room cleaning.

Although jobless, he refused to help with household work or child-rearing. However, her situation was improving. VA finally qualified him for a PTSD 100% disability pension in return for him taking therapy and medication. He now spent his days helping with the children and working with other needy vets.

Then came Marge: mousy brunette Ohioan with blonde highlights, a fifty-pound overweight, high school grad with one Down syndrome child which she blamed on her husband's exposure to Agent Orange. Some of the latest research suggested she could be right. As an Army engineer, her man had received more exposure than most. Phil suppressed his war-guilt and feelings of responsibility for his child's condition. He insisted on working night shifts. Sleeping during the day provided him with an excuse to keep from interacting with family and friends.

Emotionally numb, he spent his little free time in the basement staring at a wall decorated with his medals and pictures of Vietnam. Fearing another Down syndrome child, Phil would not have sex or be intimate.

Number three, Janey: blonde (probably natural), once fashionable now out-of-style clothing, some college, with a boy and a girl. An American classic, married the captain of the football team, sent him away to war and got back someone with a rewired brain. Jack grew upset when Vietnam was mentioned and refused any meals containing rice. A perfectionist, he lost job after job arguing with his supervisors over procedures.

Brimming over with survivor's guilt, he told her if he had only paid more attention to detail, he wouldn't have lost so many men in Nam. He now worked in the family business, whose members barely put up with his obsession. Very harsh and controlling at home, he recently broke down crying and sobbing when his son left for college. Jack felt he was no longer able to protect his son from his veteran's perception of a horrific world.

The last woman, Kathleen (nickname Pepper), told a much different story: great red hair, master's degree in biology, a two-year-old girl baby, and a West Texas accent. Married a two or maybe three tour Vietnam Army veteran – former Lieutenant Teigler wasn't sure himself. Her husband's behavior was in some ways typical of PTSD afflicted veterans. Emotionally numbed, he admitted only having enough capacity to love one person. Pepper believed this, since when he played with the child, he remained cool to her and when affectionate with her, ignored the baby. She attended family and church functions alone. Not able to stand the pressure of social gatherings — his misery obvious to all attending — Teigler would either abruptly leave or start an argument. At random intervals, he would disappear to deal alone with the weight of war-guilt and rage. Although not able to work with others, he wrote and sold stories and magazine articles, achieving a modest income and recognition.

But something very scary intruded on this relationship. At times, Pepper felt threatened and fearful when his personality seemed to change. During these periods, he seemed more alert and high energy than normal. His musculature, posture, and responses reminiscent of, and she would shudder, "…of a wild creature." Being a trained biologist specializing in lizards, she labeled this behavior *reptilian*. Sometimes this transformation would occur during intercourse, frightening her deeply. Or, as she said, "Imagine having sex with a Komodo dragon." Her family pressured her to seek a divorce, fearing Teigler might harm her or the child during one of his episodes.

After the women's therapy ended, Pepper stayed behind to relate a personal reoccurring nightmare. She lay in a hospital bed located in a smoke-hazed surreal room. A naked Teigler pinned a strange man to the floor attacking him with her Grandpa's old trail knife. The victim screamed as he was chopped apart, like one quartered a chicken for the pot. Beth arranged for private sessions with Kathleen after future group therapy meetings.

April lived up to its reputation. Bleak rain leaked out of an early evening dark sky, gained velocity, and pelted against the tall windows. Beth clicked on the overhead lights. Six very busy months had passed since her arrival. She couldn't call herself a real VA fixture yet but felt satisfied to be on the downside of the learning curve. The last appointment of the day was about to begin. At the completion of her March meeting with Pepper, the

53

two decided the next step would be a solo interview of the husband. If that went well, they would advance into couple therapy. A knock startled her out of planning mode.

Alma held open the door for the twosome, Pepper held the baby with one hand, the fingers of the other entwined in Teigler's. It had been difficult to convince him this trip was necessary, and she wasn't about to let him back out now. The man stood over six feet and likely two hundred pounds. Dressed informally, he wore a Black Watch plaid tartan shirt and blue jeans. Black Wellington half-boots matched the distressed-leather bomber jacket he held in his hands. A wide brown leather belt featured a tooled representation of a snake complete with imprinted scales wrapped around his waist. The heavy brass buckle displayed an inflated cobra head complete with fangs that fit into holes punched in the leather. The man's hair, black with some sprinkled gray, had begun a gentle retreat on the sides, which in the future would leave a widow's peak. The former soldier's face was lean and olive skinned, its best feature very deep, dark brown eyes, now alert but apprehensive.

"Dr. Mueller, this is my husband Rod Teigler. Rod, this is Dr. Beth Mueller."

They shook hands, the man, face neutral, nodded. Beth motioned him towards a chair in front of her desk. She would sit behind it for this interview, putting her in a superior, more professional position. The advantage might be needed given

Pepper's disclosure of her husband's Mensa range intelligence and the effort it took to get him to the interview. Mother and child reluctantly left to be entertained in the waiting area by Alma.

"Rod... may I call you Rod?"

A nod, he sat at attention in the chair, the jacket placed defensively across his lap and waist. "We are here today to get to know each other better and to determine whether it is time to start couples' therapy. Is that your understanding, and are you and your wife willing?"

After a pause, "Yes, I understand, and we are willing."

"Let's get started. Tell me about your life, starting with your earliest recollection advancing to the present."

🖋

Teigler, Pepper and child, and Alma sat out in the entry waiting for Beth to finish her notes. It was well after dark. Given the high-risk neighborhood surrounding the hospital complex, it would be better for them to proceed in a group to the parking lot.

The interview had stretched longer than expected, but progressed better than expected, with even a few chuckles. When she pointed out how suspicious and negative many of his perceptions were, he responded,

"Doc, throughout history, all human groups have lived with their share of paranoids. And sometimes they're right. The trick is to know when."

Teigler displayed many of the characteristics of a heavy dose of PTSD. The major ones, including anxiety attacks, flashbacks or intrusive memories, reoccurring dreams, emotional numbing, and difficulty displaying intimacy. His two and a half years in Nam had exposed him to much heavy combat. He lost friends to bullets and a fiancé via a Dear John letter. He belonged to no clubs or associations and had no hobbies, writing being his only outlet. Only one strange occurrence popped out when questioned about feelings of suicide.

"Yes, I've considered it many times. Tried it by attempting to drive my car into a truck at interstate speeds. And I've sucked on the barrel of my 45 Colt often enough."

"But you haven't been successful."

"Someone always stops me."

"Someone or something?"

"I can't really say."

"You mean you don't know?"

"I can't really say."

Beth sensed an opening to something major. She bombarded him with a battery of fast questions. His shoulders started to shake. The muscles in his face reconfigured themselves into a rigid mask. Lips parted, emitted a whisper-hiss. He twitched and twisted in the chair; an internal battle raged. Teigler gasped and relaxed back in the chair sweat-faced, the session obviously over. She tapped in a final sentence, clicked on *Save,* then the shutdown icon on the computer. She grabbed her purse and coat on the way out the door.

The foursome walked along the shadow-streaked sidewalk in a column of twos, Pepper, baby, and Teigler in front, followed by Alma and Beth. The misty cold rain collected on the surrounding trees and bushes dripping off to splat on the concrete and the walkers.

A black van caught them in its headlights switching to brights than back to low beams. It speeded up then screeched to a halt. The doors slammed open, fragments of *Gangsta Rap* arrowed through the air: *...capped him in his ass, no time motherfucker* ... Five men in baggy pants and hoodies tumbled out – one carried a baseball bat.

The women froze. Teigler reacted, spreading his arms. He forced them back away from the street towards the buildings. Between Beth's office and the hospital proper an alley opened. The women ran past a metal dumpster before stopping up against a chain-link fence. They were trapped in a cul-de-sac! Instinctively, Beth and Alma formed a human shield, pushed Pepper and the two-year-old behind them.

Beth watched Teigler back slowly into the alley, positioning himself between the men and the women. She could hear him sob, it stopped – his body seemed to swell and then compress. The shoulders came down, he leaned over at the waist, knees bent and balanced, left arm extended palm up. His body started twitching to the rap beat. The lead gang member pulled back his hood and motioned to the others, they stood back. His hand came out of a sweatshirt pocket. Beth saw a silver flicker of light reflect off an eight-inch blade. He moved low and held the knifepoint upward, sidling forward in an experienced blade fighter's stance. Teigler forced his opponent to step with the beat of the music. The two men moved with the rap, back and forth, side to side, with the grace of dancers doing an MTV video. The knifeman leaped on the beat; arm held straight, blade pointed up, aiming to penetrate up under the ribs into the heart.

Teigler deliberately broke the music's rhythm throwing the man off balance. His left hand fastened on the gang boss's forearm pulling him forward and to the side while the veteran's right hand shot up into his opponent's face. The index and ring fingers inserted themselves into the homeboy's nostrils. Teigler's body twisted using the gang member's forward movement to spin the man around in a complete circle creating a centrifugal force that tossed the body into the hospital wall. Beth heard a crackle and a short ripping sound. The man screamed. The knife clattered on the concrete. His hands covered his face. Blood gushed down; the soft tissues of the nose only attached to the bridge of his forehead by a thin string of flesh.

Teigler stooped and recovered the knife. The hood with the baseball bat lunged forward, swung the weapon left-handed. With a sinuous flexing movement, Teigler moved close inside the swing, taking the blow from mid-bat rather than from the more powerful sweet spot. His quilted leather bomber jacket absorbed some of the force, but Beth thought she heard a rib crack.

Teigler's right arm came down, pinning the bat. Instead of letting go the man leaned back, tried to tug it away. A spark of light turned into a streak as the blade in Rod's hand flashed over an exposed throat. The bat dropped to the left, the dying body to the right.

The screams of the first man continued to mix with the rap lyrics. *…blew him away, took his bad bitch…* a third gang member fumbled in his belt, freeing a short-barreled automatic pistol just as two hundred pounds of Vietnam veteran smacked into him. They rolled man-over-man on the ground twice; the pistol skittered across the alley. Beth's jaw dropped, Teigler leaped to his feet, straddling the man who lay prone and unmoving, the knife hilt protruding from his ribs. The cords of his neck protruded, Teigler bent forward and screeched at the remaining gang members. The sound like metal-tipped fingers on a blackboard. In the cold night air, a thick stream of white vapor, snot, and spit blew out of his mouth and nose. The screaming gang boss ran by the two remaining homies. His gurgling "Oh God, oh God, oh God" chant just the right rhythm, harmonizing with the music. The rest broke and ran, slammed the van doors, and left ribbons of dirty tire smoke down the street and around the corner.

Beth pulled a cell phone out of her purse and dialed 911. The beeps made Teigler spin in his tracks. He pulled the knife out of the body and rushed her. Left hand fastened on her neck, lifted her to tiptoes. The right hand holding the knife flashed forward, paused within an inch of one eye. Gangster blood dripped off the blade, ran down her cheek and stained the collar of her rain-speckled gray trench coat. If there was a hell, Beth was looking into the face of one of its denizens. She thought, *Pepper is right. It is a reptile.* A tinny voice floated up out of the dropped cell phone, *"Hello, this is 911, hello…*

Beth couldn't breathe. She pushed against Teigler's body. It was all springs and wires. Her hands clawed at his choking fingers and felt steel cables contract. Pepper shouted, "Rod, Rod, no. Goddamn it, no!" The redhead pulled at the knife hand. In Beth's side vision a rectangular black shape swung forward and slapped against the side of the soldier's head. Alma was using her purse. The berserker cocked its head, looked surprised, then confused. The purse struck again and bounced off. The man's body relaxed. His arms fell to his sides, the knife rattled on the alley's hard surface. Beth collapsed, gasped. The reptile personality was gone.

Beth sat in the back of Judge Joseph C. Walter's chambers with Alma and Pepper. Pepper stood, held the toddler to her shoulder, and shifted slowly back and forth, one foot to the other, rocking the fractious child to sleep. The judicial quarters were old fashioned with walnut framed squares forming the wainscoting, the chairs fashioned of heavy wood and uncomfortable after about ten minutes. She suspected that was on purpose, so conferences would be short. With the dusty oak blinds on the double windows closed, only a few tall floor lamps offered weak indirect light. Bookshelves covered two of the walls, their bright covers a counterpoint to otherwise dark stained woods. Judge Walters sat behind his desk facing a foursome. A detective sergeant was just completing his report. An intent female Assistant District Attorney listened beside him.

Teigler and his attorney formed a second pair. Unruly course white hair and matching curly eyebrows decorated the judge's craggy face. Food stains blossomed like mushrooms on his tie, and the cuffs of his white shirt were frayed. The room smelled of old man sweat and cigar smoke, hinting that its occupant never strayed far from its comfort.

Beth had followed the progress of Rod's case. It hardly seemed like two months had passed since he had been booked, fingerprinted, and processed by the police. Seventy-two hours later, he stood mute at the arraignment with his court-appointed attorney. Not responsive to the manslaughter and assault charges, the judge defaulted his plea to not guilty. Unable to meet the bail set, the former soldier spent his time in the county lockup awaiting events. The state news media, of course, went wild with the story. Most editorialized that Teigler's sole defense of women and children against five gang members with felony records was heroic. To his benefit, the publicity resulted in the top criminal law firm in the state agreeing to represent him *pro bono*. They would bask in the media limelight with him, gaining future business from the free publicity.

His high-powered attorney speedily brokered a plea agreement with the District Attorney, who by now despaired of finding a jury not prejudiced in the defendant's favor. Teigler's law firm pointed out how intimately the state penal code on non-criminal homicide fitted this situation. The lawyer quoted chapter 9, Section 31 of the code: *The belief that force was immediately necessary as described by this subsection is presumed to be reasonable if the actor knew or had reason to believe that the person(s) against whom the force was used was committing or attempting to commit aggravated kidnapping, murder, sexual assault, aggravated sexual assault, robbery, or aggravated robbery.*

The gang members had been in the process of attempting to commit not just one or two, but all the above. Also pointed out was that the defendant fulfilled the code's proscription of a general duty to retreat before self-defense could be considered justifiable homicide. They had retreated as far as possible before being caught in a cul-de-sac with the criminals blocking the only exit.

Teigler would get off with a slap on the hand from a provision in the law called a *Deferred Sentence*. If the judge agreed the court would acccpt thc plca and not find the defendant guilty. If Teigler faithfully complied with all the provisions in the plea agreement by a set review date, all record of a plea would be expunged, and he would not have a record as a convicted felon. He hadn't been so lucky with Pepper. The violence in the alley had crystallized her decision. Beth started. Judge Walter's bass voice cut through her mental replay of events.

"Let me see if I have all the facts. Five gang members set upon this man, three women, and a child. Men that the DA's office have long suspected of doing hit and run muggings and rapes, one such attack resulting in the death of their victim. It appears the tables turned in this instance. Mr. Teigler put up a defense, resulting in two gang deaths and one man mutilated, who you arrested later at city hospital getting his nose sewed back on."

The detective sergeant suppressed a chuckle. The ADA frowned and responded, "That's generally correct, your honor."

"And, today, we need to either finalize the plea agreement or determine whether any further action is to be taken against

Mr. Teigler for the deaths of two of our more disreputable citizens and an assault on another."

Beth saw Teigler's attorney lean forward. "Your Honor, my client is an honorably discharged war veteran, holding two purple hearts, a bronze medal for valor and the rarely awarded Vietnamese Government Distinguished Service Medal. He served over thirty months in that country and experienced considerable combat. Our soldiers are trained to kill, not disable. In the incident in question, he used skills acquired in that conflict to defend his wife, child, and two other women from the worst kind of crime. After the action, the EMTs diagnosed him with a broken finger, a broken rib, and two other ribs cracked. If any charges are pressed, my client can count on a strong almost unassailable defense.

'He is also a commercially published author. His books of poetry and prose have won national awards. I note that a copy of his first book of poetry resides on the shelf behind you."

The judge swiveled in his creaky chair and pulled out the book of poetry, studied it a moment, and looked up. "What does the District Attorney's office wish?"

"The young female ADA straightened her gray mist, three-button suit jacket and opened clenched sweaty hands. "Given the verified facts of the incident, we don't believe any jury in this community would convict him, nor would any jury in any community. Therefore, we believe a *Deferred Sentence* is appropriate."

"In checking his history from Vietnam to present there are some disturbing instances that indicate berserker reactions to high-pressure situations are not uncommon for this man. We are not sure if it is safe for him to be wandering our streets. The plea agreement contains what we believe to be a satisfactory plan."

The judge replied, "I have reviewed the agreement and the psychological profile submitted by Dr. Elizabeth Mueller. Considering the service he has done for his country and this community and the fact no charges can solidly be pressed a court order will be issued requiring Mr. Teiglar to adhere to the agreement. He will report tomorrow to Dr. Edward Waszlowski at the VA's *Psychosocial Rehabilitation Recovery Center*. The Doctor will assign a therapist and determine a schedule of regular therapy sessions and medication, if needed. A monthly report will be sent to my office summarizing Mr. Teigler's progress, a copy to be forwarded to the DA's office.

"As a further protection for both the defendant and the general public, for the next six months, he will reside in a community halfway house. At the end of that time given a positive prognosis from his therapist he will be released into the community at large but will continue regular treatment."

"Do you understand, son?"

Beth looked at Teigler's head down, slumped posture in the chair. He nodded. The man would agree to anything. In saving them he had lost everything. Yesterday, he had received divorce papers.

"Are there any loose ends here? Anybody? Hearing none this meeting is over. Son, if you feel up to it, would you sign my copy of your book?"

SUPERMARKET TAKEOUT

Prologue

A blinding repetitive high-low flash of headlights flooded the car's interior. The long blare of a truck horn shocked him out of the nightmare. By reflex, his arms twisted the steering wheel. The car screeched back into its proper lane. The air-conditioning fan blew across sweat-soaked clothes, raising a bumper crop of goosebumps. Rod shook the dream's remnants out of his head and concentrated on keeping the vehicle within the interstate's white lines.

The dream occurred again and again. It opened with him alone, staring at his reflection in the mirror-black night surface of the cabin's sliding glass doors. A shadow moved close in the outside darkness. Rod's stomach churned. A ten-foot-long reptile thing leapt up, slamming its clawed pads and scaled muzzle against the glass. The metal frame groaned and deformed with the weight. Its thin Y-shaped tongue licked the corners of the panes. Knees shaking, he collapsed through the glass, merging into the creature – two drops of liquid mercury becoming one. Their muscles elongated as they turned to stalk the adjacent farmland. The yellow-eyed head moved back and forth, flicking tongue seeking the scent of nocturnal humanity.

He pulled his attention back to the traffic. The subcompact buzzed along the interstate, another ant in an unending chain of similar-looking vehicles. The rental agency had come off a busy day, and this was all they had available. Left with no choice, the deal lubricated with a healthy discount, Rod agreed to take the diminutive hatchback.

After the first fifty miles, he uncovered its good and bad points. The five-speed manual transmission made for peppy acceleration, reaching highway speed more quickly than most of its breed. The suspension was tight, and it handled just a cut or two under the sports car he once owned. The car also lacked the syrupy nicotine smell of most rental vehicles. On the bad side, the shocks transmitted every bump, large and small, to the passengers. And it was black, a bad flannel-hot color for the Midwest summer.

He watched dark fields and small-town lights spin past, the radio on an NPR station. Janis Joplin's hundred proof, fried voice belted out a late sixties blues tune — a tribute to his lost generation — many of whom still hid in woods and wild places. He was only one breakdown away from joining them. Like the others, Vietnam had rewired his brain.

At the VA, the psych doctors said multiple personality disorder but were confused because that was only supposed to happen if you were abused as a child. Rod told them where it lived – coiled inside the back of his brain. They didn't know about the dream that came again and again.

But one of them had it right. The doc theorized a separate berserker creature, violent, cut off from all human emotion, a throwback to our ancient reptile ancestors. It surfaced and ruled during life or death situations growing stronger each time. The medication they prescribed made him feel made of wood. He quit taking it. Rod couldn't be Pinocchio, with never a chance of becoming a real boy. So, it's in there. Quiet now. Looking through his eyes… waiting.

The way he moved, back straight, measured steps, arms swinging in relaxed rhythm, caught Alice's attention. She guessed him at over six feet and near two hundred pounds. The lightness of his step, the play of muscles through the faded t-shirt and stonewashed jeans indicated he was in good physical shape.

It was difficult to tell more in the dark supermarket parking lot, the two of them moving in and out of foggy green circles cast by mercury vapor pole lights. A chill ran over her skin, contrary to the heat and moisture still radiating out of the concrete and asphalt. It had been a hotter than normal day. Taking her cold flesh as a warning, Alice stopped and did a circle, scanning the lot. They were the only occupants. Besides their two vehicles, a scattering of cars at the far end marked the employee parking area.

The quiet spooked her, allowed a bubble of fear to surface. She listened. While the man was visible, he moved silently – probably rubber-soled shoes. She reached into her purse, fingered the keys to her white VW Rabbit, paused, and then decided to continue her original errand. This was the only store open this late and it closed in half an hour – the downside of living in a small town recently evolved into a bedroom community. The moment of fear could be a premonition or just something her mind dredged up from the voracious reading of hundreds of murder mysteries.

Her footsteps started again, clicking noises marked the progress of her composite heeled shoes. Once inside, in full light and under the eyes of the staff, she would feel silly about this moment.

The outside doors sensed her presence, swished open, exposing a line of interlocked grocery carts. She tugged at one; it was stuck. A second tug failed. Two long-fingered tan hands grabbed the cart, startling her. A sharp jerk separated out the end cart. She looked up at the man from the parking lot. His forearms were hairier than most, a soft, faded brown cotton shirt molded to his chest.

She experienced a light-headed moment imagining him in a wet t-shirt contest. His eyes were very brown and very deep. Alice froze, paralyzed like a bird caught in the hypnotic glare of a snake. The cold metal frame of the cart brought her back. Older than her first guess, his age made apparent by lines and wrinkles around his eyes and lips, and black hair highlighted with random touches of white.

Exposing no teeth, he gave her a quick tight-lipped smile and turned to select a plastic red shopping basket nested in a stack near the inner door. Her sniff disclosed no distinctive scent; no cologne or deodorant – perhaps he was allergic. Wouldn't block the pheromones either. As he marched into the produce section, she noticed his leather-topped Nikes had been polished to a high gloss. Ex-military or law enforcement, she thought. The casual interest budding in her leafed out as her final calculation of his age placed him in his early to middle forties.

The conclusion: a bit alien to her small-town experience… but interesting. Lonely for a long time, she felt a visceral attraction. A well-maintained body spoke of discipline or at least good genes. Might be a bit of the bad boy there also. What to do next? She wanted to express interest but not seem too brazen. If the man felt her cat claw thoughts in his mind, he gave no indication, continuing to twist a green wire tie around a plastic bag of red and yellow striated apples. Cartwheels squeaked as she waltzed past the checkout counters, this time of night manned only by a clerk and a bag boy.

"Hey, Alice," the boy shouted. "How do you like the music?"

For the first time, she noticed that the usual elevator music had been replaced by the Classics and not Rock n' Roll classics either. "Oh, for Pete's sake, Wagner's *Götterdämmerung*, Erv must be the night manager," she shouted back. "Matty, Bobby, you'll just have to bear it."

A less than happy Matty rested a farm woman's broad backside against the checkout partition and pointed up towards the partial second floor. Alice could just see the top of Erv's head through the business office window, probably bent over the opera's score trying to harmonize with the singers. He was her second cousin and as a relative she felt obliged to listen to him try to convert all and sundry to be fans of such music. His dreams of becoming an opera star, taking triumphant tours of foreign lands, one that would never materialize in this hick town. Not that he didn't have a good enough voice for the church choir, a role that would probably be the height of his achievement.

"When you come back though, I've got some good dirt to pass on."

Matty wiggled her eyebrows. "Also, Jack Barker's been released from federal prison."

Moving on, Alice caught something more about Mr. Benson and the neighbor lady through the now booming music. Bobby picked up a folded over copy of the local newspaper and penciled in a number on the sudoku of the week. The kid, a third cousin and a numbers' genius, worked at the store during summer vacations from MIT. His often-expressed goal in life was to work out the math for a hyper-drive engine, which would allow faster than light travel to the stars.

Alice turned into the cereal aisle with the thought that everyone in this damn town must be related, except Mr. Benson and the neighbor lady. So, if they were entangled, at least it wasn't incest. Then it registered: Jack Barker out of the pen after a fifteen-year sentence. He'd been a nasty one. Worked his way up from school bully to car thief, to burglar, ending with bank robbery and assault. His last victim still walked with a cane.

She caught a flicker of motion as the tall man crossed the aisle near the meat department.

As predicted, she felt foolish from being so spooked in the parking lot. The overhead fluorescents flooded the store with soft white light bringing out the reds, blues and greens on the cans and boxes with their buy-me messages. She moved with a relaxed step, trying to ignore the music and the rhythmic squeak of one of the cart's wheels. A mélange of scents tickled her nostrils and made her mouth water as she entered the spice section. The smell grew more intense and she put a finger under her nose to keep from sneezing. Someone must have spilled pepper.

The town was lucky to have a store this large, only made possible by the interstate highway connecting them with the state capitol some thirty miles south. Over the years, suburban residential construction had crept north. The latest multi-unit commuter housing development built flush with the town boundary finally provided the density to allow the construction of a real supermarket. A glance at her watch indicated fifteen minutes left until closing time.

The store was part of a regional chain still owned by the original family, who not beholden to stockholders, closed on Sundays. She needed a few more items to tide her over until Monday's 8:00 AM certification test. Classified as an Emergency Medical Technician - Basic for over a year, she had convinced her boss to let her try for the next level, EMT- I85. This weekend was cram time.

Passing through the dairy department, the cart grew heavier with the addition of a gallon of skim milk, a few containers of yogurt, and a bottle of orange juice. Jelly and peanut butter completing her list, Alice moved up the bread aisle toward the checkout. She'd hang out talking with Matty until the t-shirt guy came through. Maybe she could think of a flirty opening to try on him. Just before turning the corner, she heard shouting over the music.

The threatening sound of male voices made her pause. She moved in front of the cart to peer around a pyramid of stacked boxes of saltines at the aisle's end. Three men had taken control of the employees. An older, grizzle-haired one was riffling the cash drawer, while an overweight dark hair with a broken nose watched Matty, standing very close. The blonde and youngest of the group stood back a few feet with a hand on Billy's shoulder. Alice glanced up at the office, noticed Erv being jerked to his feet by two others, one in a red shirt. A second baldheaded man grabbed a handful of the manager's hair smacked a pistol down on the bridge of his nose. Red shirt fumbled with something on the desk, the opera music cut off.

"Johnny," the old man by the register chuckled, "member, a broke nose'll sure make a man co-op-er-ate." The blond boy's cheeks turned pale. "Now, let's see what we got here," he said, pinning Matty's arms behind her back and securing them with duct tape. Her mouth opened. The man in front moved closer, jammed a hand between her legs. The cold steel barrel of a gun pressed into the curve under her left ear. Her intended scream lapsed into a half gasp, half sob. Bobby couldn't standby.

He leaped forward, slipping out of the inexperienced guard's grasp, an instinctive, non-thinking reaction to protect a female of his tribe. The boy's fists beat against the back of the dark-haired man. His target spun around, grabbed a handful of Bobby's clothes and thrust the gun, as though it was a knife, into the boy's body just below the sternum. A muffled "BAM", the bullet went through a lower lobe of the boy's heart and blew blood and bits of flesh out the exit wound.

Most of the splatter left a patterned spray over the front windows; some coated the blond's left arm. In the stunned quiet they could hear the metallic ting of the ejected cartridge as it bounced off the tile. The body slid off the counter to the floor. NASA would have to wait for hyper drive.

Alice opened her mouth. No sound came out. Her subconscious decided at light speed to shut down her vocal cords. Survival demanded silence. As her body shrank back, a hand knocked a box of crackers out of the stack causing the pyramid to collapse. For a few seconds, she and the three men at the register stared at each other. She turned and ran back down the aisle, abandoning her cart and purse; the click of her heels on the hard tile close together – panicky dance steps.

"Johnny!" the old guy shouted, "Get 'er! Son'a bitch, don' jus stan there."

The boy reacted to the command. The goods on the shelves blurred together as Alice picked up speed. She turned the aisle end corner at too high a speed, lost her footing and fell, slid across the floor. Her prone body thumped up against the cold stainless panels of the meat counter and lay there stunned. Too soon for her to recover, the blond gang member rounded the corner and stopped. He straightened and might have tried to say something, but any words were cutoff.

Alice's eyes widened as her parking lot companion stepped up behind her captor, right hand holding a heavy Pyrex pie dish. His arm, backed with all his body weight, swung the tempered glass plate. It caught the boy in the middle of his throat, crushed his larynx, and dropped his dying weight like a sack of potatoes. If the plate had been sharp edged, Alice thought, the head would surely have sailed off the body. She could only imagine the speed at which the dish's thin rim had connected. The blond laid choking, face turning dark, unable to breathe or talk. The man, plate still in hand, motioned for her to come.

So repulsed by the two murders coming so close together, she felt paralyzed. He stepped forward, sat the plate on the meat counter, grabbed her under the armpits, and lifted. On her feet again, her legs decided to work. Supported by the man, they scuttled towards the back of the store. They would have a few moments before the convicts found the dead boy.

He guided them through double swinging doors into the unloading docks. They picked up speed after spotting the back exit doors. The pair hit the crash bars and bounced back. It only opened a few inches. They could see a chain laced through the outside door handles. The man let her stand, shaking while he checked the overhead truck doors, which allowed entrance to the loading docks. Both were jammed.

She started to ask what they were to do. He raised a finger to his lips and hissed. Alice shivered. She wanted some words of assurance, wanted to know his name, wanted a plan. The bad guys had a plan. They weren't going to let anyone out. The store was now officially closed, and no one would expect it to open until Monday. The four remaining criminals had the perfect well-stocked hideout for the next thirty hours, plenty of time to finish off the store employees and the two customers.

She looked for the man. A light came on in a closet off the open area. Alice moved in that direction, thinking this was ridiculous, dependent upon this person she knew nothing about, not even a name. Since he wasn't talking, she would call him Soldier. Noticing a wall phone, she grabbed the handset and raised a finger to punch 911. There was no dial tone. She let it drop to swing by the cord.

In the utility closet, she watched the man study the labels on the store's gray metal electrical boxes. He pulled the levers down on the switches controlling the parking lot lights and outside store signs. The one marked refrigeration he left connected; the compressor noises would help conceal the sound of their movements. A large box packed with circuit breakers transferred power to the inside fluorescent fixtures and air conditioning. He switched the panel's master breaker off. All the lights went out. Covered with goosebumps, Alice shivered in the eerie silence and darkness.

They felt their way out of the closet. Battery-powered emergency lights flickered on. In the dimness, Soldier closed and locked the door. Picking up a box cutter off a nearby shelf, he jammed the tip of its blade into the keyhole and broke it off. Alice understood they would be safer in the dark. The pair moved back into the store.

The emergency lights cast shadows everywhere. Shadows they could move in – hide in.

Her heels clicked and echoed. The man stopped and pointed at her shoes. She nodded and noticed for the first time he was barefoot, the shoestrings of his sneakers tied together and looped around his neck. With shoes off, she slipped and almost fell, the nylon feet of her pantyhose slick against the recently waxed floor. Handing him her shoes, she tugged the garment down to the knees, almost falling in the process. It got tangled. She finally had to lie down while he peeled them off. With a low grunt of disgust, he stuffed the wadded-up hose in his pocket.

A barrage of loud talk and cursing let them know the gang was still fumbling around up by the registers, trying to become organized. As they made their way to the furthest back corner of the store, Soldier would stop and leave her to collect items from various shelves as they passed. They holed up in a corner of the soft drink section, the surrounding shelves stacked high with aluminum cans and plastic bottles of Pepsi, Coke, and generic brands of soda.

The man assembled his treasures: her pantyhose, a box of black drawstring trash bags, two 10-ounce cans of ground black pepper and a grapefruit knife. To Alice's eyes, the knife didn't look like much of a weapon. Almost eight inches long, and half its length was a round steel handle. The narrow scoop-shaped blade's curved edges were notched with small teeth and terminated in a short sharp point. Circles of light played across the ceiling – the criminals had found the store's flashlight stock.

A voice shouted. "Where the fuck is my brother Johnny?' It continued, "Gramps, you and Frenchy check out where he went, Jack and I will watch our guests. See if you can spot the woman."

Lights fluttered down the aisle, marked the two men's progress. "Shit! We found him, boss." A few minutes passed as the two examined the boy's body. "God damn, son' a bitch! Karl, your brother's dead." Grabbing hands and feet, they dragged the body to the front of the store and lifted it to the counter.

Karl played his light over the corpse. "There's no marks on him. Did anybody hear anything? How did he die? How could a lone woman do this?"

The men turned and flashed their lights outward in jerky patterns. Karl raised his automatic. "You two, get back out there and find her!" With guns held in white-knuckled hands the two moved in a slow crouch, heads scanning.

Soldier pulled a black trash bag from its box, fluffed it open and carefully poured in the cans of pepper. Partially pulling out the drawstrings, he tied them into a slipknot. Making two parallel cuts three inches apart in the right pocket of his jeans, the man threaded the knife blade in one cut and out the other – a makeshift sheath. He placed the pantyhose in his other pocket.

Bag in hand, the man rose. Alice started to get up; a hand squeezed her shoulder, pushed her back; she was to stay. The two criminals turned into the first aisle. Frenchy bumped into Alice's cart and stopped to investigate, opening her purse to examine the contents. Gramps continued down the aisle unaware he was now alone. Almost to the end, he heard his companion yell, "I foun' 'er purse. 'Er ID an' cell phone in eet."

"Bring it here," Karl shouted back.

Gramps spun around in time to see him disappear. Something black and slick slipped over his head, tightened, shut out the light. His fingers jerked. The gun fired blowing open three cans of peaches, their contents splattering the shelves and floor. His adrenalin pumped, muscles demanding oxygen. The old man's lungs expanded and sucked in black pepper. His wide-open eyes filled with the stuff. An explosive sneeze, he immediately inhaled another measure of the spice.

The gun clattered to the floor. Soft tissues were burning, burning. . . He tried to scream, running blindly down the aisle, bounced off one side, then hit Alice's abandoned cart. Body and cart spun out into the open area at the front of the store. He couldn't breathe. Gramps tore at the bag, its quilted strength stretching, resisting. He staggered a few steps toward the checkout counters, fell, and crawled; the bag molded to his face with one last breath.

Alice jumped and almost panicked at the gunshot. Thoughts of Soldier wounded or dead blew through her mind. Should she stay or find him? As an EMT she might help. She didn't want to be alone. The conflicting arguments kept her motionless. A familiar shadow materialized. She grasped his hands in relief. They felt strange, the skin dry, flexible and almost scaly. He shook as he handed over the flashlight taken from the gang member and kneeled.

Soldier choked and whispered in a little boy's voice, "It's... it's loose." She moved her lips close to his ear, "What's loose?"

The body next to her hissed, Alice massaged his neck and back. Amazingly, there was no sweat. The muscles felt like wire ropes and seemed to squirm away from her fingers. She heard shouting again. Soldier stiffened.

Karl's voice went up an octave. "What the fuck! Jesus! Is that Gramps? Who in the hell is this woman?" He shook the contents of the handbag on the counter. "Jack, hold your light here." After studying the driver's license, he said, "Who is Alice Krantzmeyer?"

"She and I went to high school together," Jack responded. "Last I heard she worked at the clinic. I can't believe she could do this shit."

The gang boss raised his head and howled, "Alice, Alice… you're dead. You bitch!

Fucking bitch!" He tore at the card. Slammed it on the floor. The men stepped back. Karl paused, wiped spittle off his chin, and regained some control. "You two go kill her. Don't come back till you do, or I'll shoot you myself."

As soon as they were out of sight, Frenchy grabbed Jack's arm. "Jac, ma grand-mere, she tell us kids bout the *whitigo*. Es person who change shape. . .kill, drink blood. I have ver' bad feelin'."

"Relax, man. This isn't some fucked up bayou swamp backwater. There ain't no gators, snakes or boogiemen. I grew up here."

"You first. I watch yer back."

Jack moved one slow step at a time, trying to be silent. He shut off the flashlight and signaled his companion to do the same. She wouldn't be able to track their movement by the glare. He noticed the emergency lights starting to dim; their batteries normally only lasted long enough to let people evacuate the store. One at the end flashed on and off. He motioned for Frenchy to keep up, the distance between them kept growing. The man must be scared shitless, he thought. "God damn you, close up."

Jack turned the corner and moved along the meat display cases. At right angles to the main aisles were several shorter rows of shelves, which led to the far wall of the building. The first walkway featuring dog food selections and pet toys was empty, the subdued light from the double-headed emergency spots reflected off the polished floor. He kneeled at the entrance to the second row and leaned forward just enough for a quick look and pull back. There was a shadow huddled in the corner! Someone touched his shoulder. He jumped, then relaxed as he caught a whiff of Frenchy's bad breath.

"Damn, don't you ever brush your teeth? All right, I'll go down this aisle, you go down the other, we'll catch her between us."

About halfway down, and she hadn't moved yet. Jack waited a few more seconds to make sure Frenchy was in place. He raised the flashlight. On the other side of the shelves, he heard shoes rasp the floor. Several short jerky scraping noises ended with a heavy flopping sound.

What the fuck was Frenchy doing, had he given them away? Jack clicked on the flashlight. The woman leaped out, flushed like the pheasants he and his father used to hunt. Startled, he fired twice, missed her, and exploded several half-gallon plastic bottles of diet Pepsi. "Frenchy," he shouted. "She's on your side. Shoot!"

Jack raced around the corner, slipped on the pool of soda, fell and broke the light.

Jumping up, he limped down the dark aisle, tripped and fell on top of a warm, still body. He felt around in panic, finding the face had a broken nose.

He found the second flashlight nearby and pushed the on button. Frenchy wouldn't ever be frightened again; his neck was tilted at an unnatural mechanical angle. Jack pulled at the strange brown loop around the corpse's neck. As it came free, he recognized it as pantyhose tightly twisted into a rope. The hair on the back of his neck lifted. He could feel eyes watching him. His companion had been right. There was a monster.

He had to escape. But Karl guarded the only way out. A decision came quickly. He'd rather kill the boss or be killed by him than stay here in the dark. Looping around the back of the store, then up through the vegetable section would put him in line for a back shot. Karl would never see it coming. Jack would take the register money and get out.

Alice squeezed in between two of the meat cases near the fruit and vegetable displays, directly under a blinking, dying emergency light. Face and right arm sticky with sprayed Pepsi, she attempted to control her breathing and slow the escalated thump of her heart. Events had moved too fast for her; the shots, the dead body and the race to escape. Where had Soldier gone? Maybe it was better for him not to be near. A man who could kill like that, it couldn't be imagined.

A shadow moved directly towards her. "Jesus, help me," she whimpered. The overhead spotlights blinked on, "oh, hell," she recognized Jack Barker.

Barker spotted a pair of feet sticking out, polished toenails black in the dimness. Jack liked them; he had always been attracted to female feet. Fifteen years without a woman, too bad he was in a hurry. He stopped. "Hello, Alice."

The emergency light flashed. She saw Soldier creep up. Flash. The knife came out of its improvised sheath, held low. Flash. Jack raised his pistol, leveled it at her head. Flash. A hand came up around Jack's face; the three bottom fingers clamped over his mouth and the thumb and forefinger pinched his nostrils shut. The two bodies came together as tight as any lovers' embrace.

Flash. The knife blade winked as it spiraled up, all four inches of the blade entering Jack's right side at an upward angle just above the belt, where Alice knew the kidney was located. Flash. She could see both faces. Jack's looked like a contorted wooden mask. The eyes of his killer glowed neon yellow, like a night creature caught in headlights.

The cooling body brushed her feet as the creature lowered it quietly to the ground. Alice got up to run. Two sinewy hands closed on her neck, cut off her air, and lifted her up on her tiptoes. Her eyes bulged; face turned red. This wasn't a man any longer. The transformation complete, it would kill anyone

86

without hesitation. The reptile paused. It was male. The head lowered, and it sniffed. The hands relaxed slightly. She took in some air.

It was puzzled. This was a female. The scent told him she was in season. Opening its mouth, it licked her cheek. The sweat contained more chemicals. The creature began to feel aroused. The female's body responded. Her temperature rose, breathing doubled. She could smell and sense its reaction.

One hand left her neck and clutched her waist, the other locked in her hair. Its lips came down on her neck, teeth nibbled. Alice let out a long gasping, "Ahhhh." The night's shock, fear and exhaustion were too much – barriers fell. Rushing up out of the medulla, primitive instincts took control. They were two snakes about to entwine into a caduceus.

A series of gunshots came from the front of the store. Bullets crashed randomly through shelves and glass cases. Reptile heads snapped around to face the threat.

"Jack, Frenchy, where are you boys? Dead?" Karl answered his own question. "They're dead!" The emergency lights faded to candlelight level. A car drove by on the interstate overpass, its high beams made a shadow race across the length of the store. Karl fired again and again. "Come get me you bitch. I've got something for you."

Dropped from the reptile's embrace, Alice lay on the floor completely confused. She watched her companion crawl towards

Karl's location. The creature's body moved, suspended off the floor on arms crooked and held out to the sides, palms down flat. Hands and knees alternately pushed, a slinking side-to-side movement. She thought it resembled the way she had seen alligators or Komodo dragons move on TV.

Something must be done; this madness must stop. Looking up at the ceiling an inspiration came. The sprinkler system! If activated it would set off an automatic alarm at the firehouse.

Damn, it was too high. She could never reach it. Alice's thought process focused. The meat department with its lower ceiling might be the answer. Pulling herself up, she concentrated on throwing one shaking leg after the other.

Just enough light remained to see the sprinkler heads. They were lower here, but still too far away. She grabbed a push broom, leaned against the butcher block and tried a swing. Not quite enough. A bullet ricocheted past. The last bad guy continued to fire at shadows.

Alice levered herself up on the meat-cutting block, stood and swung. She started giggling. It was… piñata time. She tried again and connected. The holding link broke off, pinging on the floor. Water sprayed out, drenched her, and made footing slippery. Her giggle grew, leaped into shrieking laughter. It grew louder and louder, she couldn't stop. The water-distorted demented sounds blew out of the meat department, echoed off shelves, ceiling and vibrated the front windows.

88

Surrounded by hideous noise, Karl started uncontrollable shaking. His bowels let loose. A shadow detached from the floor and leapt on him. The master criminal was too frightened to speak, move or lift his hands. His screams didn't start until teeth started working his flesh and bone, the pain immense. The man felt himself being lifted. His body tossed like a rag doll against a front window, Karl crashed through to rest on a pile of glass shards covering the asphalt. He heard a siren and saw a pair of Nikes crunch through the glass. A car door slammed, engine started, and it drove off. Moments later a fire truck and the sheriff's patrol car pulled into the parking lot.

Epilogue

Sheriff Charles Krantzmeyer stroked his bristly mustache and took a sip of three- teaspoon sweetened coffee. Two FBI agents stared at their untouched cups and the gray file folder that lay on his desk. It contained a mystery of major proportions now three months old. The agents looked almost as alike as Tweedledum and Tweedledee. Both wore dark navy suits, white shirts and red power ties. Even similar haircuts, the only difference being the older one clipped his sidearm on the right side and the younger on the left. The ancient window air conditioner rattled on, giving the illusion of cooling. Over the coffee smell he picked up the odor of Old Spice. Damn, he thought, they even use the same deodorant.

Chuck spoke up, "I believe it's time to close the file. Too many questions – not enough answers."

The head agent inhaled the stale cigar smoke atmosphere in the office. "Let's do one more run through."

The sheriff ran a hand through short-cropped gray hair. "We have one dead local boy, whose murderer has been identified. Four criminals also put to rest, and the survivors completely confused about who killed them. You fellows have the gang leader, any progress there?"

With a sour look, the junior partner responded, "Karl Berghoff is under heavy sedation and in isolation at the federal psychiatric hospital with the thumb, index, and middle fingers of both hands bitten off. Fingers we have never found, by the way. He still isn't coherent and will only say, 'Don't kill me, don't kill me!' finishing with peals of hysterical high-pitched woman's laughter."

Krantzmeyer started checking items off a list he had scribbled out earlier: "Matty, the checkout clerk is doing better, but still doesn't remember anything past Billy's murder. Erv, the night manager, from his position bound and gagged behind the counterclaims to have seen nothing, except some animal-like thing leap on Karl at the end. Alice says there was a strange man present, but outside of a very generic description does not know anything about him. Not even much about the kind of horse he rode in on."

The senior agent broke in with a grunt. "No forensic evidence of any kind has been discovered in the store or parking lot to support the existence of this mystery man: no fingerprints, scraps of clothing, blood, tire prints, etc. Only Alice's recollection that he drove a dark-colored hatchback, like millions of others."

The sheriff nodded, "Well we do have a few smeared bare footprints, but lacking a data base to search, they can't be identified. And the grapefruit knife used to take a core sample of Jack Barker's right kidney had a few threads stuck to it from a pair of generic Wal-Mart blue jeans. So, where does that leave us?"

Both agents lifted eyebrows and stared at the sheriff, their lips compressed. He pushed up straight in his chair, the casters making squeals of protest. "You can't possibly imagine my niece Alice took out the criminals. She's lived in this little town all her life, has no military or martial arts training, and has sworn oaths to save life, not take it. Oh no, there *was* someone else. Someone who, without leaving nary a trace, wiped out four full grown killers, one at a time with the most primitive weapons, in ways that drove a hardened criminal insane with fear. I'm closing the local file. This is your problem now. And if this man or creature is out there... you had better be afraid."

Dennis Maulsby

Poems from *Near Death/Near Life*
Published by Prolific Press in 2015.

THEY'RE ALIVE, ALIVE...

Thousands of years ago
they crept into our homes
to create dank and secret lairs
where they patiently plan their dirty plots.

We clean them out
but they grow again
out of the refuse.
The survivors become more
clever and cruel.

Big eat the little
to become stronger, larger.
Someday they will be ready.
From under the couches, out
from beneath our Posturepedics
they will rise.

We are unprepared
to repel their attack.
Why won't you listen?

The Mutant Dust Bunnies
are coming!

PICTURES FROM ORBIT, TUESDAY, 09/11/01

The satellite camera clicks.
In a globe of clouds and air
a tiny city shakes.
White flakes swirl in streets

between smoking glass towers.
The telephoto lens zooms closer.
Vines of fire snake-crawl upwards.
Shattered crystal eyes weep little dolls

to fall and break upon the concrete.
Stone and metal avalanche down,
sweep away men in blue and yellow.
Smoke and ash billow out,

making running people gray —
no black, white, red or brown,
a day of only one race —
they beg for a hundred years of sleep.

Stories from *Winterset*
A book of short stories published in 2019 by NeoLeaf Press.

Irish-born Father Patrick Donahey retires to the small Iowa town of Winterset. He will not find the life of books and long rural walks he expects. The community is awash with supernatural creatures. Some friendly, some not, but all must be dealt with to protect his parish, community and the world at large from destruction,

The Norwegian American Troll

This story also appeared in the July 12, 2019, issue of
The Norwegian American Newspaper.

Father Donahey, in blue-striped pajamas and ancient checked flannel robe, sat in a Bentwood rocker in the rectory's screened-in back porch. A gentle breeze murmured through the netting, bringing the mixed aroma of lilac, azalea, and peonies. Donahey took a sip of heavily sugared coffee and reflected upon his state of mind and body. A curl of smoke rose from the pipe on the side table. His physician and his psychologist both were trying to break him of smoking.

Of course, they, Dr. Bhramari Gupta, physician, and Dr. Catherine Darcy, psychologist, never personally experienced human weakness, since they weren't human. The first was an immortal Hindu wasp goddess and the second was the younger sister of Joan of Arc and a witch of the European model. Father Donahey realized they were trying to help him both personally and with his mission. However, it wasn't like he had volunteered for this work.

The church hierarchy had also played a deceptive role. Supposedly, he was Winterset, Iowa's retired priest, only helping when full-time Father Brown was ill or out of town. It wasn't the life of books and long rural walks he had expected. The community and the surrounding area were awash with supernatural creatures. Some friendly, some not, but all had to be dealt with in order to protect his new parish and the wider world from chaos and destruction. The mantle of guardian had been forced upon him.

The last six months had been short of major paranormal intrusion, except for a brief scare. Sheriff Rick had shared with him suspicious sightings of a homeless person who had established residence under the 106-foot-long Hogback Covered Bridge, spanning the North River on Douglas Township Road. Farmers along the waterway began to report cattle mutilations.

The lawman possessed a sixth sense when it came to awareness of mythological creatures. The man himself, another denizen of the Madison County supernatural scene, lived the secret life of a Pooka, a shape-shifting Irish wraith. The destructive nature of his demon personality was kept in check by his oath of office. He would serve and protect the citizens of this county as long as the vow remained in effect. Donahey shuddered to think of what might happen if Rick was defeated in an election and released from his bond.

Waiting for a dark night, the two of them had set up a stakeout near the bridge. After letting the night settle around them, the sheriff slipped out of his clothes and transformed into his favorite Pooka-shape, a coal-black stallion. He would be the bait, while the Father crept behind with a net and the Sheriff department's taser gun.

Lightning bugs flashed from air and grass tips. Crickets played raspy leg violins. In horse-mode, Rick grazed his way up to the riverbank. Head lowered to guzzle water. He became as vulnerable as all herd animals when drinking. A rush of water and a dark amorphous body exploded out of the riverbed. Long arms grasped his neck, moonlight reflected off a pair of long off-white tushes.

With a speed unexpected from a normal equine, the Pooka reared and twisted its neck.

The attacking creature's jaws missed and shut with the sound of a screen door slamming. Muscles convulsed; the horse's head flew back. The attacker spiraled into a somersault. Its heavy body smacked into the earth, well away from the river.

A startled Father Donahey fired the taser into the right buttock of the black stallion. It grunted, quivered, and fell to its knees. Face in a guilty grimace, the priest spit out his favorite cuss word, "Cornflakes!"

He tossed the net. This time he ensnared the correct victim. The creature squealed and rolled, almost throwing off the web of polyethylene rope. Donahey leaped and hugged the being's pillow-sized hips, keeping it from escaping.

Water squeezed out of its body hair soaked the priest's clothes. The smell of rusty river bottom, aged fish slime, and bad carnivore breath washed over him. Arms became numb and aching. A heavy, unclothed human-scale body bumped next to him. The sheriff had recovered in time, grabbing the creature around the chest. He twitched and swore, discovering it had breasts. It let out a recognizable female scream.

Father Donahey chuckled. "I think she has misinterpreted the intent of your naked attack.

Now to be sure, I won't be telling anyone about this if you won't be telling anyone about my bad aim."

The two women doctors had taken the subdued prisoner in hand. After an examination, they reported the creature to be a thousand-year-old six-foot-tall female troll. One of the northern Scandinavian Huldrefolk variety, she possessed a more human-like body and features than the southern Germanic breed. The exceptions being upper and lower three-inch-long self-sharpening tushes, the muscular development of a weightlifter, waterproof fur, and a four-foot-long tail. Her face, hands, and feet were free of hair. Her ears were small and her nose large, but within the range of human features. A shave here and there, a dress to hide the tail, better language skills, coaching on manners, and she could pass.

After deciding the troll couldn't be turned loose to prey on the local livestock, and possibly humans, the group placed her as housekeeper to the rectory. In this private household, she would learn English and social skills. Her name, in the garbled ancient Norwegian she spoke, translated to thorn bush, so they named her Rose.

Bright and adaptable, Rose quickly gained proficiency in language and manners. Her female counselors had excitedly arranged visits to the hairstylist, cosmetician, and shopping trips to West Des Moines' Jordan Creek Mall. The women, as excited as if it was Christmas, hauled in packages containing plus-size fashions from Chicos, Gap, Old Navy, Talbots, and even Victoria's Secret.

Father Donahey clicked his tongue and shook his head. Rose entered, dressed in a flower- print calf-length day dress. He noticed she had shaved her legs.

"More coffee, Father?"

Donahey was worried. He paced back and forth in front of the parlor's double-hung windows. Her still-made bed proved that Rose had been out all night. The ancient grandfather clock in the entryway struck ten, and still no sign of her. A car door slammed. He pulled the drapes aside. Walking up the sidewalk came Rose, escorted by Sheriff Rick. He rushed to the door and pulled it open.

The sheriff waved. "Not to worry, she's all right."

Rose entered, wearing tight blue jeans, a long-sleeved beige western shirt, and a modern take-off on cowboy boots. Mud coated the boots and stained the trousers up to the knees.

Donahey looked her up and down. She blushed and bowed her head. "My child, where have–"

Sheriff Rick interrupted, "Rose, you go get cleaned up; I'll talk with the father."

Given an out, the troll-woman sped off. The two men walked through the house and into the privacy of the garden.

"Well, the good news is that our girl can party." Donahey's eyebrows went up.

"Here's the story. I received a call of an altercation at The Cycle Shop, you know, the bikers' bar out at the old Swensen place. When I arrived, a concerned Knut Helgesen relayed the events. He had met Rose Wednesday in the checkout lane at the Fareway, engaged her in conversation, and asked her out to celebrate hump day with him."

Donahey nodded; he could see the attraction. Knut was one of Madison County's 450 Norwegian Americans. A Wegian troll would feel at home in that group.

"At any rate, they rode his custom Harley out to the roadhouse last night to meet with his biker group, the Thor's Hammers. After several hours of drinking and dancing, a rival gang, Loki's Daggers showed up. Not long after, the bad blood between the two bands degenerated into violence."

Donahey grimaced. "She didn't...?"

"Use the tushes? No, just fists, elbows, knees, and feet. With a whoop and a roar, she leapt into the knots of struggling men, and without regard to sides started laying them out."

Grabbing the sheriff's arm, Donahey choked out, "Any serious causalities?"

"The worst was a broken jaw, but there were plenty of black eyes, bruises, and cracked ribs." Rick laughed. "And, a whole lot of admiration. It was the most fun they'd had in ages. So, no charges were pressed, and Rose was made an honorary member of each gang."

Donahey looked back at the rectory. "What about Rose?"

"She had fled, afraid her true nature would be revealed. I picked her up two hours ago on a gravel farm-to-market road just off County 34. No apparent damage, except for scarred knuckles."

"And the bottom line is..."

"With a chuckle, Rick responded, "Well, there are about fifty guys who desperately want to date her. They'll be a plague on your house."

The Kitsune Wedding

First time in print bonus story from the world of *Winterset*.

Fresh out of the shower, a towel knotted around his hips, Father Donahey stood before the chest of drawers in his room. He opened drawer after drawer, finding socks, shirts, jeans — both regular and flannel-lined — but no underwear. Water began to drip off the ends of his uncombed hair and run down his back, causing a tickle.

He stomped over to the door, slung it open, and shouted, "Senora Gutierrez, where are my shorts?"

A cheery voice replied, "In the top drawer to the lef', jus' behin' the stockin's. Also, Sheriff Rick is waitin' in the library. I am servin' hem coffee and *biscochitos.*"

Donahey turned and slipped on the wet floor. He caught himself before losing his balance. He muttered his favorite swear word substitute. "Cornflakes!"

The jockey shorts he pulled out were new, straight out of the package. It was unnerving how well the new housekeeper had sized things up and put things into order – both the old two-story rectory and he and Father Brown. They had never been cleaner, better fed, and clothed. The dusty corners and dirty dishes the two bachelors had ignored prior to the new housekeeper's hiring were things of the past.

His mouth filled with saliva thinking of the Senora's *biscochitos*. The Mexican cookies ingredients being flour, eggs, anise seeds, cinnamon, sugar, and even a shot of brandy. He was forbidden from taking alcoholic spirits by doctor and psychiatrist, but the slight brandy flavoring in the cookies gave him a sneaky feeling of pleasure – as if he was a teenager finding a legitimate way around a parental prohibition.

A second thought surfaced. The sheriff rarely made social calls; Irish shape-shifting demons were introverts. His visits coincided with serious paranormal threats to the community. One leg half in his pants and momentarily off balance, Donahey danced across the floor. He flopped butt-down on the wrinkled bed and managed to sheath the other leg. He slipped feet into slippers and tucked in his shirt while heading for the stairs.

Old oak treads creaked and groaned under his feet as he descended. Donahey ran fingers through his loose almost completely white hair. He turned and entered the parlor. Sheriff Rick sat on the couch sniffing the vapor rising from his teacup, a puzzled look on his face. His large brown eyes took in Donahey's half-state of dress. He sat the cup down untouched and smiled.

"Good Morning, Father. Things must be looking up. My superior demonic senses report you are cleaner and smell better than usual."

Donahey took the chair on the other side of the table, holding the refreshments and put on some forced cheer.

"Are you here for business or just want to chat?"

Rick glanced around and satisfied they were alone answered. "I have come into some interesting information you should know."

Donahey poured tea, lemon, and sugar into a cup. The cup in one hand and a cookie in the other, he leaned back and composed his face into the neutral mask he wore during confessions.

The sheriff horse-snorted, "Be careful with those cookies, they have quite a bite. If I didn't know better, I would think John Barleycorn made them himself."

A munch on one of Senora's *biscochitos* brought a burn to Donahey's throat and nostrils.

It tasted like a sponge soaked in brandy. He gulped and quickly swallowed some tea. The brownish liquid smelled heavily of alcohol. The taste was too good. All his suppressed desire for booze flooded his brain. His hand shook as he dropped the unfinished cookie into the cup and set it down hard enough to make the saucer rattle. He fought off the temptation to gulp the whole pot. Senora Gutierrez and he would have to have a talk. No way would he drop back into alcoholism.

He interlocked his fingers to stop his shoulders and arms from shaking. Donahey forced himself to speak.

"So, my bucko, what's so important to interrupt a man's morning ablutions?"

Sheriff Rick wrinkled his lips. "I was out last night, just taking a pleasant gallop by moonlight, when I met a fellow spirit in a strip of woods east of North River – the other side of Hogback Bridge road."

"This was in Pooka horse-mode, I presume. Looking for mischief, were we now?"

Rick clicked his tongue. "Father, you know I am bound by my oath of office to 'protect and serve.' Just getting some fresh air and galloping away my boredom. At any rate, this fellow, comes up and introduces himself. In fox form, he was. Initially, I mistook him for a wild critter."

Donahey wrinkled his brow. "A fox spoke with you. Suren you had been grazing on a rogue marijuana patch in the woods."

Rick smiled, exposing spade-shaped teeth. "Right. Shame on you, Father, for even thinking of such a thing. Oh, it was no regular fox. A *kami*, an ordinary Japanese spirit, of the variety known as a *kitsune*. Very polite and high-status fellow with nine tails. He was bearing good and bad news."

105

This was it. Donahey had felt itchy and nervous for the last week. Something paranormal was coming. *Nine tails?* He stayed silent, rather than show ignorance.

The sheriff leaned forward, one hand on Donahey's nearest knee. "There is going to be a wedding. A couple of royal fox spirits will exchange vows tonight at Pammel Park. I've been asked to provide a few deputies to close off the park and guard the entrance."

"Why would they want the service here? I only know of one person of Japanese origin, Rioku, the wife of Gunner Thorson."

"Actually, that is the main reason. She is a fox spirit. I guess it's not entirely uncommon for human men and kitsune females to marry. They're shape-shifters, you know — can appear as whatever they want — a beautiful woman in this case. Thorson and she fell in love, when he was stationed in Okinawa with the Marines. Her younger sister will be the bride. Secondly, the Ley line gate in the park allows easy arrival and departure."

"So, why are you telling… "

A terrible thought hit Donahey. His face puckered up. " – they don't want me to perform the service?"

A husky atonal cackle of demon laughter filled the air. "No! They are Shinto/Buddhist, not Christian. The family just wants absolute privacy for the ceremony. Anyone disturbing or even watching a kitsune gathering will be in big trouble. At a minimum cursed, at the maximum dead."

"And how will you keep folks out? 'Tis a public park after all."

"Well, I am opting for a wildlife scare. We've had confirmed sightings of cougars in the northern and central parts of the state. Wild boars and brown bears come across the border from Missouri."

"You put out a bear is roaming around and every camera-nut in a hundred-mile radius will be storming in."

"Not if the phantom bear is thought to be rabid."

Donahey rubbed his forehead. "Well, that might work. So, what is my part in all this?"

Sheriff Rick rose and headed for the door. "No part. Just wanted you to know before your third eye detected their presence and you decided to investigate. They mean no harm. You stay away."

He stopped, turned, and adjusted his trooper hat. "By the by, a number of them in human guise will be visiting the John Wayne Birthplace and Museum prior to the wedding. Seems like the Duke has a lot of fans among the supernatural."

Donahey waited until the sheriff was ten minutes gone, then took the large leather-covered paranormal creature book down from its shelf. He sorted through the pages until arriving at the 'K' section.

Kami – Spirits described in Shinto/Buddhist literature. Maybe elementals, such as forces of nature; revered ancestors;

or other supernatural manifestations. Kami possesses good and bad characteristics and behaviors. They rarely interact with humans, preferring to live a hidden complementary existence that mirrors the real world.

Flipping through several pages of examples, Donahey arrived at the sub-definition he sought.

Kitsune – The Japanese word for fox. These creatures are intelligent and possess paranormal talents. Kitsune maybe tricksters, evil witch animals, or may take the roles of protector, friend, paramour, or spouses. Their abilities, power, and the number of tails — to the quantity of nine — increase with age and wisdom. After achieving the maximum of nine tails the spirit's fur turns gold colored. Supernatural abilities include shapeshifting (plants and animals), pyrotechnics, possession, intruding into others' dreams, and driving people mad.

Warning: Kitsune enjoy imbibing alcohol and can do crazy things while under its influence.

As a member of Alcoholics Anonymous, Donahey certainly understood the full implications of the last sentence. The book slipped in his lap, closing with a loud slap. Dust motes from its dry velum pages swirled in a beam of multicolored sunshine coming through the library's circular stained-glass window. He rose, replaced the book on its shelf, and left for the kitchen to talk with Senora Gutierrez.

He pushed through the full-size swinging door and entered the kitchen. A familiar smell assaulted his nostrils, one which raised the hackles on his neck. A glass bowl sat on the counter. Donahey approached, bent down, and sniffed. The liquid in the bowl was in large part red wine. Chopped onions on the cutting board suggested that the noon meal would feature some type of French soup as the main course.

A moment of temper rose. He spoke out loud, "I thought I made it clear to the Senora that no alcohol was allowed on the premises."

He glanced around for the housekeeper/cook, then began opening the cupboards. Staring at him from the shelves were bottles of various shapes and sizes holding liquors: gin, vodka, rum, tequila, whiskey, and wines. A gallon container sported a label bragging 190 proof pure ethanol. His body reacted, mouth drooled, desire for the products of the distillery burned in his body and mind. Anger and frustration built. He remembered the intense brandy taste of the cookies. What the hell was she trying to do?

"Senora Gutierrez. Senora Gutierrez!"

Her name echoed off the high cream-colored ceiling's stamped tin ferns and flowers. Donahey straight-armed the kitchen door, took the stairs two at a time, and headed for Father Brown's room. Huffing and puffing from the exertion, he knocked. No response. He listened at the door and heard snores.

Opening the door, he found his colleague flat on his back, legs hanging over the bedside, pants down around his ankles. He leaned over and caught a whiff of his breath. The man had passed out last night trying to change for bed. A coffee cup on the bedside table reeked of spirits.

Donahey shook his shoulders, eliciting a moan. This was wrong. While Father Brown took a snort now and then, he was no big drinker. The forbidden booze squirreled away downstairs, the spiked tea and cookies, and the full-time priest incapacitated. It made no sense. A door opened and closed downstairs, its hinge squeak and closing slam identified it as the back- porch screen door. He descended the stairs as quickly as a creaky seventy-year-old could, being mindful of the danger of a fall.

In the kitchen, his face masked in a frown, he confronted Senora Gutierrez. She stood staring at the bottles exposed by the open cabinet doors.

"Senora," — Donahey waved his left hand towards the booze — what is the meaning of all this?"

Her black-to-the-bottom eyes glared into his. She pulled the green and off-white *rebozo* shawl from her shoulders. The tassels, knotted into the shapes of tiny rabbits, strummed against the floor. Donahey gasped. Her facial wrinkles and jolly cheeks thinned and grew smooth, the white in her salt and pepper hair became black as obsidian. The breasts and hips grew more youthful and slender. Carmine lips snarled – her exhalation one of pure two-hundred proof ethanol.

Every internal alarm, physical, emotional, and supernatural, blared in Donahey's spinning mind. An adrenalin surge allowed him to brush the creature aside and storm into the back porch and then out through the screen door. He ran through grass, dodged around flower beds, and raced for the gate in the back fence.

Something flashed in his peripheral vision, he tripped on something warm and fleshy.

Landing face-down, he flipped over and sat up. Donahey blinked several times, thinking he was hallucinating. Charging towards him was a horde of rabbits – flamingo-pink rabbits! *I must be drunk,* he thought. *But shouldn't I be seeing pink elephants?*

A wave of ruddy bodies washed over him. Donahey kicked and punched. Rabbits flew up. More piled on. He sank back under the accumulated weight. Fur pressed against his eyes and nose. His body forced flat, Donahey's panicking mind did the math. Individual rabbits only weigh four pounds or less. To keep his one-hundred-eighty pounds constrained there must be at least a hundred of them.

Hot rodent bodies sealed his mouth and nostrils. Unable to breathe, he panicked. Donahey shook and twisted. No opening to outside air came.

He woke feeling bruised, confused, and still confined. Eyes popped open. He tried to stand and failed. The chair legs under him screeched on the linoleum floor. He gasped, remembered the fur pile, and, for a moment, thanked God he hadn't suffocated. Donahey found himself in the kitchen, his chest, arms, and ankles immobile. Rough woven ropes of some natural fiber bound him to a chair. He squirmed, eliciting more screeching noise.

"Well, well, well, padre, struggling is useless. I have braided those *cuerdas* out of the body and leaves of my sacred maguey."

Recognizing a supernatural creature, Donahey tried to call on the trinity. He could produce nothing but mumbles. A wad of the maguey fiber-filled his mouth.

"*Cabra vieia,* old goat, you didn't think I would allow you to invoke your God?"

Donahey wiggled his eyebrows and pointed with his chin at what should have been the housekeeper.

"So, you wish to know who I am. My name is Mayahuel, the Aztec goddess of the *metl* plant or what is known as maguey in your language. Its gifts are many. Its fibers make the rope that binds you, thorns can be used for needles and the skin covering the leaves for paper. But the best gift is that of the drinks — mescal, pulque, and most recently tequila — made from its white juice."

A growing thought brought horror to Donahey's mind. He slammed his body back and forth. The chair squeaked and groaned. His captor grabbed the arms and kept it from tipping.

"Now you are beginning to understand. *Maldito*, you have been too successful. We have been attacking your strengths. This time we attack your weakness. The *cocone* — my children — the four hundred rabbits surround and guard the house. Your fellow priest will not waken for hours. We will not be interrupted."

Donahey resisted. The only part of his body unbound, he tossed his head back and forth, up and down, avoiding the goddess's attempts to force liquor down his throat. Most spilled and dribbled down his front, soaking his clothing. A spoonful or two made it past his defense.

The familiar burn down his throat and the sweet smell in his nostrils brought forth the suppressed fanatical desire for the drug his body and mind craved. It argued for him to give in to the promised bliss. He slapped it back.

Mayahuel grabbed a handful of his hair, pulled his head back, and forced a white plastic kitchen funnel through the mush of maguey fibers in his mouth. A rush of tequila flushed into his mouth, pressure built and… like a dam breaking, the flood washed down his throat. It seemed like only seconds before tingling, sparking pleasure raced through his veins to curl his fingers and toes.

Releasing his hair, his tormentor tossed an empty bottle to smash and send shards skittering across the checkered linoleum floor. She reached for a full one. "Ha! So, it begins. Let's see just how much of a drinker you really are."

Donahey moaned. The goddess grabbed an ear and pulled his head into position, Clear liquor glugged out of a fresh bottle, filled the funnel and overflowed. He gulped and gulped – all resistance ended. The alcohol took possession of his body. A great wave of hot laughter welled up inside him. His body shook with it. Donahey wanted to grab the beautiful woman and kiss her. He took a deep sniff, she smelled like growing plants, desert tar bush, mesquite, sage, and, of course, maguey.

A horrendous crash interrupted, Donahey could feel the shock wave up through his feet.

A ringing rumble of hoofs grew louder and closer. He heard a stallion's screaming challenge. The half-empty bottle flew out of the bitch-goddess's hands. He tried to turn his head to see what was coming behind him. The chair and he flew into the air. The heavy wood of its frame breaking into its component parts.

He smashed into Mayahuel, forcing her airborne. She sailed out the back door to crash supine onto the lawn. A black velvety muzzle pushed him over. Donahey spit out the gag and funnel. He roared with laughter to recognize the Pooka. Ankles still tied; its head thrust between his knees. A toss of its neck sheathed his lower body like a wreath around its neck.

Facing backwards, Donahey's belly and chest lay flat along the giant horse's back. His arms free now, but still tied to the broken-off chair arms, grasped the creature's sides. The Pooka spun and raced back the way it had entered. Donahey saw the bitch-goddess rise and signal her minions. A flood of pink rabbits sprinted after them.

Through the blur of their passage, Donahey noticed wrecked furniture, scattered books, and the rectory's oak door hanging on one hinge, its oval clear glass window spider-webbed with cracks. The Pooka had forced a surprise entry. Rose-colored rabbits waited outside lined up like pins at a bowling alley. The fifteen-hundred-pound Pooka hurtled through. Four-pound rabbits flew outward at odd angles, except for three, which remained in their original positions, their bodies mushed into hoof prints, dying legs still twitching.

From his rear view Donahey spotted a rough column of Mayahuel's ruddy fiends on their tail. He giggled, "Better go faster, pretty horsy."

Hoofs pounded on the concrete street of a residential area. A small sober portion of the priest's mind tried to determine which animal was faster, rabbits or horses. Such non-magical animals could both do up to forty miles per hour. Paranormal creatures would probably be faster, but proportionally the same. The Pooka and the *cocone* would be evenly matched for speed. He hoped his steed would have more endurance.

The sun shone only inches below the treetops. *It must be around half past six in the evening*, Donahey thought. Local folks would be home and at the dinner table, and not watching this parade through the streets. Bouncing on the raised spine of the horse, his abraded chest and belly reminded him of why saddles had been invented. The adrenaline rush and the heat of the wraith's body had taken the edge off his drunk. He felt both disappointed and grateful.

Street signs flashing by allowed him to determine they were headed southwest. Reaching the outskirts of town, the Pooka picked up speed. The pack of rabbits drove hard, legs bending and stretching, bending and stretching. The Pooka kept ahead, but the pursuers maintained their distance. Donahey wondered what the sheriff-pooka had in mind. Eventually, even supernatural creatures would tire and like ants swarming a much larger grasshopper, the rabbits would take them. With rodent teeth and claws they would dismember them both.

He felt a swell of drunken affection well up for his pooka-buddy. Donahey tried to express his love, but his alcohol numbed lips could only mumble. His ride seemed to understand and let out a long whinny and shook its head.

The rabbit horde was closing the distance. He felt the horse change gait as it entered a wooded area, leaving the asphalt road for a hoof-soft path. Branches scraped along Donahey's bare arms. Disturbed burr oak leaves released a musty, tannin smell.

The Pooka went airborne, sailing over a fallen tree — the rabbits ran under — gaining. Up they went again and again, a regular jump course. Donahey's stomach gave up its contents, spewing over the Pooka's right hip.

Getting rid of that load helped him sober up. He could identify the details around him.

His ride was slowing, he saw white foam flecks on its flanks. His nose picked up the acrid smell of horse sweat – his shirt soaked with it. The *cocones* were at their sides, leaping to bite and kick. Yellow ichor trickled from wounds in the Pooka's hocks and cannons. One rose-colored lapin leaped and sank his buck teeth high into the thigh of the Pooka. The demon's heavy wild tail swept it off.

Donahey began to pray. Hundreds of rodent teeth would soon mince them into tiny pieces. The black stallion broke out of the tree line into a clearing. Donahey's eyes swam with shimmering blurred colors, golds, blues, reds, greens... The devil horse raced through an open area. On one side Donahey caught sight of a man and a woman standing before a Shinto priest. The woman wore a pure white *uchikake* kimono with matching *tsunokskushi* headpiece. The man wore a shorter black *haori* jacket over *hakama* gray pants. Facing the trio, stood at least a hundred watchers.

Oh God, he thought, *we have violated the sanctity of the Kitsune wedding. Worser and worser. They will curse or kill us all.*

The Pooka stopped, spun, and faced his rodent enemies. They came to a full stop to the left side of the assembled kitsune. Nothing moved. Donahey felt his steed's lungs repeatedly fill and empty.

As though a signal had been given, the kitsune in mass reverted to their fox shapes. Silk kimonos of every color and shade collapsed, flattened on the meadow grass. Multi-tailed foxes attacked. The rabbit pack exploded. Pink streaks dispersed, scattered, and blew away in every direction.

Donahey laughed. *The foxes are fresh, the rabbits are already exhausted – no contest.*

Taking advantage of the melee, the Pooka trotted off into the forest.

*

Three days had passed. He had been drying out, attended by his Hindu goddess physician and his witch psychiatrist. Their potions and magic had beaten back the craving once more.

Mayahuel had accepted defeat and retired with what few of her rabbit children remained.

Carpenters had re-hung the front door and repaired the other damage to the rectory. The cover story released by the sheriff's department was that one of Iowa's numerous white-tail bucks had been chased into town by hunters and seeing its reflection in the rectory door window had attacked. Supposedly crashing through the entrance, the one-hundred-forty-pound animal ransacked the interior in a panic before busting out the back door. Such rare intrusions happened periodically throughout the state, lending credence to the false report. The few townsfolk that had caught a brief glimpse of the chase were herded to the psychiatrist and eased of their memories.

He sipped black coffee and wondered what revenge the kitsune would wreak on the Pooka and him. After all, Sherriff Rick had purposely led the pink rodent mob into the midst of the wedding. A knock at the rectory entrance broke his chain of thought.

Opening the door elicited a gasp. There stood the sheriff and a shorter man dressed in a kimono embroidered with lucky cranes. The autumn sun reflected off the green shimmery silk. The man had golden hair, a long-pinched nose, and a sharp-toothed smile.

"Father," the sheriff spoke, "the honorable prince Akio would like a moment of your time."

Donahey's eyebrows went up, his knees suddenly felt weak. The two took his silence for ascent.

"Father, I wish to present the thanks of the bride and groom, the wedding guests, and myself for what you have done for us."

Clearing his throat, Donahey rasped, "Thanks? I thought we violated the peace of the wedding."

The two demons chuckled, their bass and tenor voices blending. The kitsune continued. "The wedding was about to face a disaster. The confused caterer had delivered the entire wedding feast — drink and meats — to the wrong location. To Winterville, Georgia rather than Winterset, Iowa. Bringing wonderful rabbit for each guest to catch and eat saved the honor of the event. Especially since each of the long-ears were marinated in alcohol."

Donahey's hands twitched, his eyes blinked. Sherriff Rick picked up on his puzzlement. "Father, the *cocone* eat, drink, and breath booze. Their blood tests out at 190 proof. That is their nature as minions of Mayahuel."

The prince nodded, bowed, and said, "Please let us gift you this robe as a token of our appreciation. *Domo arigato,* and now *sayonara.*"

The robe deflated and draped over the steps as the man inside shapeshifted. A golden-haired, nine-tailed fox scampered down the porch stairs and around the corner.

From *Near Death/Near Life*
Published by Prolific Press in 2015.

OMAHA BEACH

Against the moon
rest sharp-cut shadows
of bluffs and scrub trees.
An inbound breeze
unleashes the memory
of gun oil and wet canvas.
The wandering voice
of Judy Garland
creates throaty notes.
A milky tide pulls sand
from beneath my bare feet.
Around me, spirits cluster,
field strip weapons, chew gum
and talk in Jazz patois.
More gather,
arriving from all
the compass points.
From the high ground
comes a tinkling piano
version of Lili Marlene.
Reaching critical mass
the spirits burst out
of the surf,
run, crawl and twist

across the beach.

Hundreds fall –
scattered shredded leaves.
The rush breaks
and hesitates
at the foot of the bluffs.

Gathering strength,
clawing, pushing,
lifting each other,
they flood over the top
to vanish in the sunlight
of a new day,
drawing in their wake,
the crashing
triumphant boogie
of a thousand Big Bands.

Note: This poem was set to music and played on National Public Radio for the Sixth Anniversary of the WW II Normandy landings. Go to www.dennismaulsby.com for the musical rendition.

Stories from *The Assisi*
An unpublished novel

The Assisi follows the life of a man 250 years in the future after a worldwide apocalyptic plague. The illness and the resulting breakdown in governments and societies all over the world have reduced the population by over 90%. Most of the story takes place in the old USA central Midwest. Survivors clustered around people who knew how to provide food and shelter without high technology, basically the Amish, Quakers, Indian tribes, an abbey, and other green communities.

The hero (Billy) is a ward of the state (Council of Ministers) and as such is being fostered for four years at a time in various communities. This story takes place during his time with the evolved Native American tribes.

THE WEDDING

The groom's party of companions rode down the trail cut by the rub of many years of traders' iron-rimmed wagon wheels. They rode their finest, most pampered ponies. Palominos with gold fur and white manes and tails. Appaloosas, wearing splashes of brown or black over white undercoats. And many painted horses with broken-colored coats (also known as piebalds and skewbalds) formed a brave procession prancing with ears up and heads held high.

The men, however, slumped in their saddles, their faces peaked pale reflections in the mid-morning sun. Hands holding the reins of their many-colored ponies shook a bit despite their efforts to will them steady. The horses sensed this weakness and took advantage by tossing heads and resisting direction.

The men of several related villages had collected for the party held the last night of the traditional three-day bachelor hunt, bringing jugs of their favorite recipes of brewed *tizwin* corn beer, honey mead, and the fermented mare's milk called *kumis*. Joints of rabbit, deer, and raccoon — fruits of the hunt — roasted on spits.

Aged arthritic ones sat, swigged, and tapped out dance rhythms on drums. The young and more spry oldsters danced and sang. The blotchy-faced full moon floating overhead witnessed the strange behavior and kept its silence as it had since time immemorial. The air was filled with smoke and sparks from the fires. The smell of dancers' sweat mingled with the spicy barbeque sauce being brushed on cooking meat. During rest breaks in the festivities, Billy listened as jokes and ribald stories were bantered about. The married men and worse, the inexperienced unmarried, all had advice for Billy, many times contradictory about marriage and how to handle women.

He received the traditional present of a jar and a sack of beans from his blood brother. "Put one bean in the jar for every time you make love during the first year of marriage." Brow related. "Starting with the second year, take one bean out each time. There will still be beans in the jar when you die an old man."

The old men beat on the drums for one minute.

Sees Far told the story of a man who caught a magic fish.

"The fish spoke and begged to be released saying, 'I can grant you a wish in payment.' "

"Give me ten thousand horses." the man replied.

"Wish for something else," the fish said. "I'd have to steal all the horses from all the villages for hundreds of miles. It would start wars. Besides you could not feed and keep that many."

The man thought. "As a child I was obsessed with the hedge master's stories of the paradise of Hawai'i, build me a bridge across the sunset sea to that wonderful place."

"*Tsakak*! Who do you think I am? I'd have to strip the entire world bare down to the stones to make a bridge that long. It would take years to complete. You might not live that long. Ask for something else."

The man frowned then smiled, "I know. I've always wanted to understand women. Give me that knowledge."

125

The fish remained quiet for a very long time and then looked up from the bottom of the canoe. "How wide do you want the bridge?"

The drums beat wildly. Josh *itaki* rose and spoke.

"A man says to his friend, "I haven't spoken to my wife since we got married.

His friend responds, "Why not?"

The man says, "I don't like to interrupt her." The drums rattled.

The best counsel, as always, came from Bull: "Husbands must be a help to their wives in all things. Many will talk against it, saying such men are slaves to their mates. However, witness for yourself, those who live and eat well are the ones who help their wives."

As usual at these events, most overindulged and stayed up too late to make much of a recovery in the morning. Cold-water wash-up and servings of mild cornmeal mush sprinkled with bitter powdered willow bark helped reduce headaches and soothed touchy stomachs.

Buffalo hide bags containing the groomsmen's rarely worn ceremonial garb were opened. Men groaned as the bright colors hurt their squinty eyes. Flower garlands were draped over the top of the feathered, painted, and bead-worked clothing and copper-studded horse tack. Spring blossoms, gold from dandelions and alexanders, blues from prairie violet and blue flag iris interspersed with the red of prairie smoke and scarlet globe mallow were strung with buffalo bone needle and tendon thread into necklaces called *lay-eez.*

Billy felt Shadow, his crow companion, land on his shoulder and peck at the two shiny gold earrings in his left ear. He shouted, "Hi-up," moving his mount from a walk into the next faster gait. Moans and groans came from the more hung-over members of the party. The thick bundles of flowers decorating both man and horse shook as the animals trotted, releasing a concentrated complex fragrance carried by the wind before them.

Billy straightened his back, tightened his legs around the appaloosa's barrel and relaxed, allowing his body and that of the horse to become one. The animal knew the way and needed no guidance.

His thoughts drifted back. It seemed that events had moved so fast. He felt he was not ready for all this. As an apprentice medic he had recognized the signs some months ago. Among them: morning nausea, swelling breasts, spells of tiredness, and cravings for sweet then sour foods. Changes in Lily's body and behavior told the age-old story.

Billy confronted her one day when she returned alone with water from the river. "Dear one," he started, then stopped. His facial expression allowed Lily to catch the confusion and the question forming in his mind.

"Yes," she said with a quiver, moving forward, wanting him to hold her.

In his arms, her warm tears ran down his chest. She confirmed his diagnosis; "You will be a father in the spring."

He felt both fear and pride at her confirmation, having never known his own father he had no example to go by.

"It's my fault. I took no precautions." He felt the heat of her blush against his skin. "There were no children from my first marriage. I wasn't sure…"

Billy tried to lift her head up to look into her eyes. She resisted.

"You can't be obligated." She spoke in a voice muffled against his vest. "I know that you must leave in a few years. My family and I will raise the child."

He rubbed the small of her back with one hand and stroked her hair with the other. His mind stopped whirling; he knew what must be done. "Doesn't this tribe believe in weddings? Let us do the best we can for as long as we have."

Lily's shoulders shuddered, tears storm-burst, and sobbing began. Billy felt his own eyes grow wet. The pair swayed together.

Chief Bull tried to get in the mood; this should be a time of rejoicing and pride. His headdress made of a buffalo head complete with horns slipped over his forehead. The brown and white painted pony was beautiful, but its trot was jarring. He adjusted the wooly hat and wished it could be tied under his chin, but that would not be dignified. His thoughts returned to the wedding.

As usual, Lily had messed up the plan chasing her own ends. Born as a very late child to his parents, she had been scandalously spoiled. As guilty as they, he followed his parents in smoothing her path both before and after their passing. According to the plan, which Lily knew as well as anyone, Billy was to marry Baby Eyes. The two women, however, had conspired together.

The pair had approached him after they were sure Lily was pregnant and only two choices remained. The man could marry Lily, and that would be that. Or, they had proposed a second alternative.

"Father," Babe said, "it is our desire that we both marry Billy."

Bull fuming internally over Lily's earlier admission of motherhood had to listen to her request twice before he understood. His chin dropped, and he opened his hands allowing his best pipe to fall into the fire. He managed to recover some composure in the time needed to pull his treasure out of the flames. Babe rushed to present her arguments before he could refuse.

"In days not so long ago, many families consisted of two or more women and one man."

"Yet, that occurs when for various reasons the number of available men doesn't match the number of women," Bull replied.

"You planned on having the gift of two or more children from Billy before he left. This way allows for more than those few."

Bull returned to his original argument speaking one word, "Brow."

The two women laughed. Lily spoke. "No worry there, my brother. We have arranged things with him."

Before the chief could speak, Babe continued. "He became angry at first, his envy and jealousy making his eyebrows very red indeed. But we reminded him of his future obligation as Billy's brother."

Bull raised his head. Brow had always been a possible candidate for marrying Babe after Billy left for the university. But the bachelor couldn't be sure of Babe, even with Bull's blessing or urging, she might choose someone else. Then it hit him. According to tribal tradition and law, as Billy's official brother, Brow would have the duty of marrying his brother's abandoned women or finding them new husbands. There would be no competition.

The two women nodded as they saw Bull recognize their solution. "Brow thinks this will work well. He wishes to remain free of family obligation for a while, but will be ready to settle down when his brother leaves in three years."

Bull went over the women's solution again and could think of no objections. It was almost too neat. Who could have predicted that the two boys... men would forge the bond that made this outcome work so well? The reaction of the eligible men, especially Brow, to a mating of Billy and Babe had been his greatest worry. He wondered whether some divine hand worked this clay.

"I will talk tonight with your mother," he nodded to Babe, "her counsel will help make the final decision." Let them sweat overnight, he thought, that will give me some payback for their plotting and my blistered pipe.

Lily and Babe left the lodge with neutral faces. Ten paces away, they clasped hands and tried to smother giggles. What they hadn't given away: his wife Star had been the chief plotter for this whole affair. She would act surprised tonight and reluctant, finally allowing Bull to convince her.

*

Breakfast over the women hustled everyone out of the lodge, pulled down the buffalo hide door covering, and left Bull and Billy sitting cross-legged by the fire. The chief kept his head down and pulled at his ear lobe, a gesture that only his wife and

131

sister would have recognized as an outward sign of internal guilt. The boy-man across from him had no idea of how he was being manipulated.

With an effort to stay dignified, Bull asked, "Does Crow Arms wish counsel with me?"

"I… I wish to talk with you about ma… marriage."

"Marriage?"

"Yes, your sister Lily and I wish to marry."

Bull did a poor job of looking surprised, which went unnoticed by the nervous suitor. "How does she feel?"

Licking dry lips, Billy responded, "She is willing."

"Hummm," Bull pretended to ponder. "I am not sure I should give my permission." Billy looked stricken.

"She would constantly nag you to do things her way, has a foul personality, and may be too old to bear you children." Bull detected some movement around the fire hole in the roof of the earth lodge. He had better watch his language, since they were being spied on.

Billy gulped, "I don't think the last item is true."

There was a distinct rustle overhead. The boy would pay for that. "Anyway, given the small pool of eligible men, Baby Eyes should be married first. Lily has already had her chance with a previous husband. Why don't you marry Babe?"

The boy choked and nearly fell over. A barely suppressed giggle came from above. Bull waited to see if Billy would pass the test. "Give me your answer."

The air grew a bubble of deep and expectant silence, to include the listeners around the smoke hole.

"I would marry Lily," Billy said resisting temptation. He did not know his mother or father. He had made a vow, repeated many times during lonely dreams that he would never abandon a child of his making.

"You have chosen an honorable path. But that leaves us only one solution," he looked upward as though invoking *The Old Man That Lives Forever*, "you must marry them both."

This second shock created a riot of swirling thoughts, some pleasant, some not. "Would they agree to this? Would the tribe agree? What about my blood-brother Brow's desires?"

Bull recognized Billy was still thinking in this matter as a Quaker or Amish. "None of those involved will object. Most all are hoping you would agree. The two women have lived and worked together all their lives. They do not wish to be separated. By our law, Brow is already responsible for the education of your children and stands to inherit your wives when you are called to the university and beyond."

Sweat formed and collected on Billy's forehead and cheeks. He clasped his hands together to keep them from shaking. The muscles in his throat tightened making his response raspy, "I will marry the two women."

Bull thought he heard the rustle of skirts and the sound of female hands coming together.

Now, I must ask the hard questions. "How will you support this new family? You are not a hunter, and we cannot ask that you kill game when it is against your nature."

"I have thought this out, Uncle. My gift will allow me to capture and train wild horses. Indian horses know only three gaits, mine will know five and will fetch much in trade." In truth, Billy had other trading schemes in mind also.

"I am glad you have worked this out. The wedding will be held under the new moon of the fifth month. There remains only the setting of the bride price."

"Bride price?"

"Surely you did not think that you would get these jewels of women free. This family would lose all respect if no price or a low price was paid."

Billy remembered the pairings of the last year. Five to seven horses or equal value in furs and goods seemed to be the going rate. He waited.

"I would set the price as follows: twenty horses for Baby Eyes," Billy's eyes widened, "but... only ten horses for Lily since she comes to you slightly used." Bull heard a muffled gasp fly down from the smoke hole, he would pay for that, but he couldn't help getting in a little dig at his willful little sister. He let the silence build.

Some little pieces of bark and rolled pellets of dirt fell from above into his lap. One bounced off his nose. He let all the parties sweat for a few more seconds.

"However, your actions during the chase of the Comanche raiding party allowed us to regain these women, so in honor of the debt we owe you, the price is halved. Fifteen horses or equal goods to be delivered before the next complete moon cycle will clinch the bargain."

Billy responded as they grasped hands, "Yes, Father.

Bull stared into the fire. Billy and the listeners were gone. Rarely alone, he savored the moment. Concentrating on the bark and rolled earth pellets, he watched them rise into the air on invisible hands and form into a ball over the hottest part of the fire. It burst into a blaze; he made the fire dance in patterns. His secret gift: to lift and move things with mental energy only. Billy, the animal empath, was getting into more than he knew. Lily could start fires and Babe… a new gift to be hidden from the monks and shaman, could see inside things. As a little girl she knew the best walnuts, the ripest fruit, and when the corn was exactly ready for harvest. Recently, she had described to Lily what the baby inside her looked like. It would be a boy, she said. Bull wondered what gifts the children from this double match would possess. It would be better not to guess.

BILLY AND EB CONDUCT TRADING DAY.

The rising sun looked only a hand-span above the horizon when they finished unloading and displaying the wagon's goods on wooden drying platforms. Located in an open meadow outside the village, the racks were normally used during the harvest season to dry corn and squash in preparation for winter storage.

Indian men and a few women leaning forward under high-stacked backpacks stabilized with headbands were the first to arrive. Almost on the heels of their moccasins came those leading ponies and dogs harnessed to loaded travois. Billy looked closely. Two poles were crossed and tied together just above the animal's shoulders; the other ends spread to form the legs of a 'V' dragging on the ground. Ropes secured the poles to the animal's chest and back; a platform of crossbars stabilized the rig and carried the cargo.

Besides trade items, people brought lodge poles and hides for teepees, baskets and containers of food, bundles of dress-up clothes and on some rode shouting and wiggling children. Evidently, most planned on staying the night or several. People,

137

ponies and dogs continued to accrete until they all blended together into one milling mob, packing the meadow to capacity.

Men brought buffalo robes, hides, and composite hunting bows complete with bound sheaves of fletched arrows. Furs of all colors and sizes were held out for inspection. Some presented handfuls of almost pure copper nuggets received in earlier trades from northern tribes. Artists showed off both scrimshawed and plain boars' tusks. One lucky individual had several pounds of metal scrap dug out of an old ruin. The iron would fetch a good price, the aluminum bits basically worthless since no one knew how to work that metal anymore.

The women traded decorative clay pots, tanned deer leather aprons, and dried fruits. Eb was particularly interested in jugs of recently collected maple syrup and shelled walnuts, chestnuts and hickory nuts. Many offered waterproof bark boxes containing rose hips and dried leaves for teas, such as Comfrey, Fireweed, and Sweet Goldenrod. Others unpacked stem-tied bundles of medicinal and fragrant prairie plants.

The males usually left with iron arrowheads, knife blades, and linen shirts to be embroidered by wives or mothers. Also high on their lists were brass studs and shiny broad headed tacks for bow and tool decoration and wooden toys for sons and daughters. As always iron hoe and axe heads remained popular items with women, more efficient than their bone and chipped stone alternatives. Other domestic purchases included cast iron pots, steel needles, scrapers and awls. Billy spotted the youngest daughter of Bull, his blue-eyed, raven-haired greeter and mud partner approaching and moved to place himself in her path.

"Good morning, Baby Eyes," He said. Eb had explained that many of the tribe's children were born with blue eyes, most of which turned brown or black during their first year. Rarely did one of them retain that color.

"You call me Babe, cousin," she said, coming to a stop beside stacks of blankets. Her fingers rubbed a thick, tightly woven white wool blanket with four broad colored bands at each end.

"Would you trade for one of these?" Billy ventured.

"This is a lucky one. The colors give it power: green means new life, red for hunt, yellow for harvest and blue for water." Babe held it up under his neck to measure against him. "Too small, you will be big man." She laughed, a most wonderful husky sound.

The size of an individual blanket was marked with foot-long inch wide indigo stripes, from one and a half stripes for the smallest to four for the largest. She separated a three striper from the pile. "This will do, how much? Maybe, I make you a hooded coat from this one before next winter."

Completely disarmed by flashing eyes and the promised gift, he settled on a too low price. She folded the blanket, placing it in a large basket atop earlier purchases of needles and off-white linen thread she would dye herself. Her attention switched to a display of combs fashioned out of cow and ox horn, selecting one of the few left with very narrow spaces between the teeth. These had been selling well.

"Why are these so popular? We're almost sold out of this kind."

"Lice," Babe replied. "When people live close together for the winter. . . "His new cousin left the sentence for him to finish. "We comb them out."

Billy's head immediately started to itch. He reached up to scratch, remembered the humor in her voice and lowered his hand.

"Not that kind." She pointed to his crotch, "The other ones."

Now he felt a most terrible itching sensation. Fingers trembled and clenched, but he managed to cancel the automatic reaction to move them to the threatened area. He would have to wait. Babe sauntered over to Eb by the wagon to pay for her purchases. Billy failed to catch the trembling in her shoulders or the repressed grin on her lips.

From *Near Death/Near Life*
Published by Prolific Press in 2015.

GRANDMOTHERS' DANCE

Standing in a circle, they discuss the errors
their children are making as parents,
and despite the mistakes,
the perfection of their grandkids.

You watch the grandmothers sway
from side-to-side, one foot to the other.
It's a reflex, a habit they say, echoes
of all those years of rocking babies,
of comforting sick children.

It's a gentle waltz, with no apparent music,
insinuated into our ancestors from time spent
in ancient trees swaying in the slow breeze
of an eon-old African evening.

A dance more primal than Salome
shedding seven veils — a pattern of steps
that draws you back to memories of warm arms,
the soft silk pillows of women's breasts —

your small sleepy head at peace.

The Sommelier
An unpublished novel.

It's modern times and yet many of the old gods still exist among us. Dionysus and his girlfriend Terpsikora, the muse of dance, live in New York City. With thousands of years of experience as the god of wine, he works as a master sommelier, and she as a prima ballerina. What else? But, it's a cover for their roles as independent contractor-assassins for the CIA.

THE BURGLAR

As Denys and Kora, they travel the world undercover. Denys working at five-star Michelin restaurants, consulting with vintners, and conducting workshops for master sommelier candidates. They are fussy and only accept CIA hits with minimum risk. Their idyllic life is shattered when Kora is kidnapped. Denys is given a new partner and sent on a chain of violent suicidal assaults trying to rescue his lover. Kora always seems to be moved just before his arrival. He begins to wonder if there is more to this than a simple kidnapping. The following extract introduces the novel's main characters.

The man's body flowed smoothly around the shadows of furniture. Making little sound, only the small circle of his flashlight beam predicted his progress. He'd gotten by building security dressed in a typical cable repairman uniform of brown shirt and khaki pants while waving a formal-looking work order. Once past the guard, instead of fixing the fictional outage in apartment 1803, he proceeded to the penthouse. The two simple locks on the door took three minutes to defeat. He wondered about the absence of better precautions-especially no alarm system to complement what was primitive lockage.

Whoever owned this pad needed a serious upgrade. This assignment was no challenge to his skills. Born with the potential to only achieve five feet in height, he had compensated for his short stature. He had become sneaky. Learning many ways to move through and around things had allowed him to avoid the bullying members of his hood. In addition, he could fight back, entering their homes to leave little gifts in their beds or in the boxes of cereal in their cupboards.

As an adult, he had turned his increasing sneakiness to profit. A ten-year string of successful burglaries ended when a moment of weakness with a betraying bitch of a woman had landed him a prison term. In his second month of hell, a government man from some alphabet agency had recruited him. The ensuing work had been exciting but nowhere near as profitable.

Stepping up on a chair, his mini-drill buzzed, making a hole for the combination wide-angle camera and microphone. Per orders, he would install the micro-miniature bugs in the bedroom, kitchen, study, and deck. He'd put a device of his own in the bathroom. He grinned. You never knew what goodies you might see.

The short man slipped through the hallway and entered the kitchen. Copper and stainless-steel pots and pans hung from hooks along the top of a butcher-block topped island across from the wall containing the sink, stove and fridge. Backlighted by city glow shining through the glass wall facing the roof garden, a long low shadow slinked across the top of the island.

What the hell, the intruder thought.

Sweat formed on lips and underarms. He moved the flashlight like a pistol. A pair of slanted eyes glowed with reflected fire. His hand jerked away and then returned to focus on the pointed ears and pear-shape of a seated feline.

"Whoa, just a cat." he murmured to himself.

The creature unbundled itself. The human noted dark spots and stripes and a size about twice what one would expect of a normal housecat. In the circle of light, the cat opened its mouth and hissed, sharp-pointed fangs seemed finger long. It leaped.

The man screamed and bounced off the counter behind him. The flashlight clattered to the floor. Shouting "No, no, no " the fake cable guy ran for the door. Another scream as a second black stalking shadow attacked. The apartment door slammed as the intruder made it to the safety of the elevator entryway.

A pleasant sun warmed Denys' meat and bones. Dressed in a red silk kimono decorated with cherry blossoms, he relaxed into the memory foam cushions of a beige rattan chair. His entire body felt like one slab of sore muscle. He had forgotten that Kora and her sisters had collaborated on the *Kama Sutra*. She had pushed him to the limit of his physical capabilities and a bit beyond. He reminded himself not to bet with her for at least a month. Denys sipped from a chocolate-colored Noritake coffee cup. The Hawaiian Kona coffee cleared his throat and nostrils. He sat the cup on a glass-topped rattan side table to rest alongside a companion breakfast plate covered with a napkin.

The twentieth-floor rooftop garden and apartment were places designed for serenity and rest. Dwarf eucalyptus, miniature crab apple, and mature tulip trees provided shade for beds of creeping thyme, bleeding hearts, hydrangea, and primroses. In partial shade and sunny areas grew the raw materials of his profession: mini limes and oranges, heritage tomatoes, chicory, cherries, and grapes. On one wall basil, fennel, ginger, and mint tumbled out of pots. Multiple entwined gazebos wrapped in flowering vines shaded the remainder of the outdoor deck and the stone-wrapped pool.

The glass wall separating the garden from the apartment was broken only by a circular bar, which could service both areas. It's interior much resembled the cockpit of a modern fighter jet, agleam with glass and chrome instruments and machines of the mixologist's trade.

Denys heard the approaching shuffle of bare feet and the scrape of leather-soled shoes. "Sweetie, look who I found at the front door."

Turning, he watched Kora enter dressed in a red and blue batik-dyed sarong. The skirt began above the knees, rose over slim hips, and draped over one shoulder. The arrangement left one breast exposed, but modestly covered by her now unbraided long hair. Typical of Kora's style, a pink nipple peeked through with every other step. The man's face following her matched its tint. Denys felt gratitude. She was softening up the visitor prior to their negotiation.

Denys put on a pair of silver-mirrored sunglasses. If you couldn't see a person's eyes it was more difficult to read their reactions.

The reluctant host waved a hand with spread fingers towards a matching couch. "Well, Mr. Jones. Please take a seat. Always glad to deal with the ubiquitous Joneses and their guests. Have trouble with the Smiths, though. Glad you chose the better name."

The Jones sat and pulled up the knees of his gray tropical wool slacks, a habit among those whose usual dress was a business suit. An ivory-colored short-sleeved shirt with the beginnings of sweat marks covered his torso. Since it was only

147

warm and not hot, the wetness on back and armpits denoted his discomfort and anticipation of forthcoming events.

The man was trying to hold a poker face. Carefully shaved cheeks, thin lips, and dull brown eyes seemed relaxed. A breeze fluffed the man's average-length brown hair. A pale hand with fraternity ring instinctively lifted to pat the left-side part. The totality of Jones's appearance was designed to be forgettable, to be able to move through crowds on the street, in cafes or subway without creating a memory.

To the more astute, however, Denys noted the agent had made a mistake. The man's eight hundred-dollar Burberry wingtip brogues gave away his economic status besides being too formal for the outfit. Sandals, given the weather, or even loafers would have been preferable and more forgettable.

Oh, well, he thought, *Jones is an administrator, not a master of disguise.*

Silence stretched out. Unhappy with last night's break in and sure of who had ordered it, Denys waited. He watched Jones's lips quiver. They were dry and chapped. The man was probably thirsty, but there would be no offer of refreshment until an apology was offered.

Under his host's staring scrutiny, the man shook his head and shoulders. "We've got an assignment for you."

Denys clasped the arms of his chair and leaned forward. "And here I was waiting for an explanation."

Jones rubbed his hands together, interlaced his fingers, and held them in front as if they were a shield. "An explanation?"

Scooping up the covered plate from the side table, Denys yanked off the napkin. Three tiny devices of metal, glass, and wire, lay on the plate, looking like de-shelled mechanical shrimp.

"It was one of those periodic things." Jones's hand came up to rub his cheek. "I told them not to do it."

Denys beckoned with his fingers for more information.

"The agency conducts a five-year review of all assets and contractors. Your file is a puzzle to them. Your earliest job with us dates back to 1944 when we were the OSS. Since then, you have done something for us every year – that's over seventy years. Yet we know so very little about you. No date of birth, no knowledge of parents or family, educational background, and no trace in the official records of any government or business."

"Are you and your masters not happy with my work?"

"It's great. A better success rate than any of our other assets."

Denys' lips curled. "I am not an asset of yours or anyone else's. I will accept being an independent contractor."

"At any rate, information about you is extremely difficult to come by. You have no home phone, cell or landline, and suffer no internet connection. Your mail is minimal and strictly concerns business. You successfully lose the tails we place on you. In addition, based on our scanty records you must be at least eighty to ninety years old and show no signs of aging. Hence, the last-ditch attempt to bug your domicile."

Jones was sweating profusely now. The wet cotton fabric of his shirt stuck to his sides and chest. Denys realized the man had been given an almost impossible task. The higher-ups had screwed up, and Jones was expected to patch it up rather than lose a high performer.

The sun was beginning to broadcast an uncomfortable heat. Denys decided to remain connected to the Agency for a while longer. He rose and went to the bar.

"How is your burglar?"

"He will survive, but he has more stitches than a rag doll. Claims he was attacked by furry spotted monsters."

Denys shoveled ice cubes into two tall glasses. He filled his with Perrier water and lemon slices. Still feeling an angry edge over the attempted bugging, he filled Jones' glass with quinine water and lemon slices. Unless you had developed a taste for the British invention, the bitter liquid would pucker your tongue.

Denys looked up. "They *are* monsters. Check the mosaic at your feet."

Denys watched Jones examine the scene picked out in colored stone, glass, and gold. It was a full-size reproduction of a depiction of a laughing vine-wreathed naked man leaning back in a gold chariot pulled by two African lions. Drunken women in various stages of undress followed waving grapes and wine cups.

Denys smiled, exposing spade-shaped teeth. "I couldn't keep lions here – much too big for the available space. So, I have their miniatures, ocelots."

Denys remembered he and Kora opening the door and turning on the lights. The two cats greeted them with leg rubbing. Like normal domestic cats bringing in a dead mouse, they proudly dropped the electronic gear at the master's feet. The pair found the evidence of the burglar's flight, although the cats had licked up most of the blood spots.

Jones had a flash of an old memory of a TV mystery program where a female detective kept an ocelot as a pet. "Our man was attacked by ocelots? He was bitten in the armpit and the calves."

"Ocelots size up their prey and decide where to deliver a killing bite. Your man — what's his name, by the way? — ran into Chico Malo, the male, and Besador, the female."

Jones looked around at the swaying branches and hoped it was the breeze. Denys began to feel some pity for the man.

"Don't worry, the cats are nocturnal. You won't see them today."

He reached for a bottle of pink sugary syrup to cut the bitterness in his guest's drink.

Jones leaned back in the chair and let his head relax on the back cushion. "Who's the funny dick in the chariot?"

An eyebrow raised and lips tightened, without using its contents Denys screwed the cap back on the syrup bottle. He brought the glasses back to the chairs and handed the bitter one to Jones.

"The man is the Greek god Dionysus, or Bacchus if you prefer the Roman name. He is the God of the vine, grape harvest, wine, and theater." Denys pulled off the sunglasses; his eyes grew wider, eyebrows arched. He locked his vision together with that of his guest. "You should also include among his capabilities those of religious ecstasy and ritual madness."

Jones tumbled into the eyes. He found himself in a parkland of scattered trees, ankle-high grass, and multi-petaled white and yellow flowers. He shivered. It was cool and he was dressed in a brown fur strapped over one shoulder that flowed down to barely cover his hips. The low temperature caused his scrotum to wrinkle, pulling his family jewels closer to his body – he obviously wasn't wearing any underwear. A wreath of grapevine sheltered in his hair, which now was full of tight curls. His feet were clad in what was known as Jesus slippers, flat inch- thick leather soles with straps that laced up the calves.

The sound of screaming came from below him. Small figures raced up the hill. Their ratted long hair and body parts exposed by disheveled clothes identified them as women. Long bare legs stretched and scissored.

A deer ran before them. They were tireless. It wasn't. The women caught it. They tugged on its limbs. Their mouths bit at its neck. The creature let out a bleat-squeal. Limbs broke off its body. The mad ones bathed in the blood. One spotted him. She shrieked and pointed.

Jones realized he had witnessed something he shouldn't have. The demonic women ran towards him. He turned and fled. Fear marbled his blood. It wasn't enough. The women formed an open 'C", formation – the ends engulfed him. He tripped. Jones felt long broken fingernails pierce his skin. His body writhed. Legs were pulled apart. He screamed. His last sight before fainting: his bloody testicles gripped in the hands of the insane maenads.

Excerpts from *The House de Gracie*
A novel soon to be released by NeoLeaf Press.

Nous servons, que nous soyons servis. (We serve, that we may be served)
de Gracie family motto

In the novel, twenty-eight-year-old Army Major Hugh de Gracie returns for the first time in a decade to his five-hundred-year old family home in the Adirondacks. He is dying from wounds and an untreatable virus acquired as a Taliban prisoner in Afghanistan. Kept ignorant by father and family during his childhood and teenage years, he does not realize the true nature of the family residence and its enigmatic relationship to his kind.

The family serves and is served by their domicile, the de Gracie chateau. The house is a living plant, whose human companions have evolved over tens of thousands of years to function as symbiotes to the "Mother-tree." The Major's fighting in Afghanistan has earned him an implacable human enemy, one whose culture insists on vendetta. Fahad, a Taliban commander backed by the vast resources of a wealthy Saudi family, must seek revenge for Hugh's killing of his relatives.

AMTRAK DREAM

The train jiggled on its suspension as it ran over a curved section of track. Hugh opened his eyes – the Hudson River glided by. He was on his way home to upstate New York after receiving a disability discharge from the Army.

His route had included Germany to New York via C-130, taxi to Grand Central Station, and now, the last leg by train. All modes of travel had allowed little chance for a peaceful sleep. On top of it all, Hugh was still plagued by a virus caught in Afghanistan – generating alternating bouts of fever and chills.

The clickey-clack of the train, a man's baritone rumble across the aisle, and his fever put him to sleep. Hugh drifted off into a resurrected memory.

He was on patrol with Sergeant Murphy. The pair drove a Humvee, the fifth and last vehicle of the convoy taking supplies to an outlying Afghan patrol base. They passed time telling each other riddles. Known as *Riddler,* Murphy could spew forth an inexhaustible supply, especially dirty ones.

"What's a mixed feeling?" the three-striper asked. The answer: seeing your mother-in-law backing off a cliff in your new car.

Hugh gave her one. "What is the definition of Macho?" The answer: jogging home after a vasectomy.

"What is the difference between oooooh and aaaaah?" the sergeant inquired.

After a respectable silence, Hugh said, "I give up."

"About three inches," came the laughing response.

An IED exploded on the lonely stretch of road, flipping the lead vehicle onto the roadside.

Its fuel tank ignited with a bang. Hugh bailed out of his tail-end Humvee, Beretta in hand.

A 7.62 round from a Dragunov sniper rifle struck him smack in the middle of his chest. The impact slammed him into the hood of the Humvee. He dropped to his knees. The pistol fell onto the red-brown earth of the roadbed.

Murphy ran over. She started dragging him to cover. A second round caught the sergeant in the unprotected area below the armpit. The slug tumbled through both her lungs exiting on the other side.

Face in the gravel, Hugh heard the bass chug-chug-chug of the Ma deuce fifties, and the tenor chatter of the M-240s mounted on the remaining vehicles establish fire superiority. Three minutes later, the action ended. A woof of wind blew around the vehicles, sucked up fine particles of dust to mix with black ash and the odors of burnt pork and cordite.

The ceramic plate in Hugh's armored vest had saved his life. Other than temporarily knocking the wits out of him and a saucer-sized bruise, there was no damage. He rode back to base holding Murphy, keeping pressure on the bandages while bloody foam bubbled out of her chest.

They failed to find the killers. The Dragunov rifle, with its PSO-1 telescopic sight could hit accurately from 800 meters.

Hugh woke, the deep tearing vacuum of her loss in his heart, with the train taking on passengers at the Albany station.

Monkey See, Monkey Go

"I think I see a koala bear down there."

Lieutenant Lewis Clark de Gracie almost lost his grip on the helicopter gunship's stick.

He turned to face Dale Grabowski, his warrant officer co-pilot. Assuming an exaggerated Aussie accent, he said, "I think you are about four thousand miles off, mate. Now, if we were farther north, say close to the Chinese border, we might find some pandas."

Dale twisted the ends of a red handlebar mustache, "But I'd really like to see those cute little koalas."

Lewis shook his head; it was difficult to determine when his second was serious or just screwing over his mind. He chose serious. "This is the Central fuckin' Highlands, my man. You need to improve your grasp of the local geography. I have a copy of the U.S. Army Area Handbook for Vietnam in my footlocker. It's yours when we get back to Kontum."

The gunship platoon normally flew support for the Republic of Vietnam and U.S. troop operations, but today targets of

157

opportunity took precedence. Intelligence sources reported an increase in North Vietnamese Army supply and troop movements into their sector. The Central Highlands, an area covering 18,600 square miles of up and down terrain (600 to 7,280 feet), were considered essential by both sides to the domination of South Vietnam.

Lewis scanned the rainforest below and checked the chopper's place in the platoon's staggered trail formation. A glance to his right confirmed the status of the unit's mascot, George, a dusty-brown rhesus macaque monkey. The young primate measured eighteen inches long and weighed fifteen pounds.

In six months with the men, pointy-eared George had bonded with the group, eating corn flakes with raw egg, rice pudding, and locally grown fruit in the mess hall and getting drunk on the Vietnamese brewed *Ba Mu'o'i Ba* beer served in the enlisted men's club. After a few beers, the monkey's fur-less pink face would turn red.

George squirmed and let out a *chit-chit-chit*. The macaque looked like a little soldier, clothed in a set of tailor-made olive-green fatigues. The maintenance folks had created and bolted a facsimile helicopter pilot's seat, just his size to the chopper floor. Tugging at the straps securing him to the chair, George curled lips to expose teeth and cut loose a long multisyllabic monkey sentence.

"Dale, the monk wants food."

158

A handful of lychee nuts dropped into the mascot's lap kept him busy. Lewis smiled when he looked at the parachute wings recently sewn on the mini-uniform. After a four-hour bout of drinking, the unit had decided to let George earn his wings. Someone had secured a miniature hand-made silk parachute to the macaque's back. The men marched along the runway to the three-story control tower chanting *"George, George, George of the jungle. Watch out for that tree."* The screaming monkey sailed off the tower's balcony. The chute inflated. He touched down and ran up a tree just off the airstrip.

Lewis vocalized his thought. "Boy, George was really pissed after his first jump."

"You said it, El Tee. Took us an hour to coax him down from his perch. Hey! Did you see that? I caught the flash of a face in the tallgrass clearing to our right."

"Rattler flight leader, this is Rattler five, enemy activity in the clearing below. Over." This is Rattler one, Rattler five, and six recon clearing. All other units follow me. Out.*"

The two tail-end gunships descended to treetop level, increased speed, and blew over the open space. Lewis's eyebrows lifted, "Whoa, Dale, the place is crawling with NVA – at least two companies out in the open."

Over the next twenty minutes, the six gunships exploded 2.75-inch rockets into the tree line. The ordnance killed stragglers and pined the majority of enemy in the open. Making passes at different angles to confuse the target, they raked the hapless troops with fire from side-mounted dual M6 machine guns. Door gunners shot up enemy officers, NCO's, and crew served weapons.

Leaders dead, isolated NVA soldiers lost unit cohesion. They dropped weapons and ran, stumbling over windrows of their comrades' bodies.

On Lewis's fifth pass, a smart-ass on the ground got off a burst from his AK. Copper- jacketed slugs punched through the chopper's duralum alloy skin to damage the hydraulic system.

"Rattler one, this is Rattler five going down. Over."

The chopper crunched into the middle of the clearing, rattling the teeth of the crew. Overhead blades geared down, reducing vibration through the airframe. Their steady *whopwhopwhop* dropped to a hum and then to a swish. The pilots and crew felt exposed and vulnerable.

"Rattler five, this is Rattler one, a heavy lift helicopter and two slicks with infantry will arrive in fifteen mikes to bring you back. We will fly cover until bingo fuel. Over."

"Roger, Rattler one, can we order a beer and pizza delivery? Out."

Dale clipped a leash to George's collar, drew a Smith & Wesson .357 revolver, and exited. Lewis followed, struggling against the aircraft's forty-degree sideways slant. The door gunners fired bursts of six rounds at any sound or movement

160

among the scattered mass of intertwined bodies. They weren't about to allow a wounded but still alive enemy to take a last-minute shot. Lewis jumped out of the cargo bay .45 automatic at the ready, discovered the helicopter's strange lean due to one landing strut resting on a three-foot pile of bodies.

Streamers of smoke from burning trees and brush fluttered across the clearing. They carried the nitrate smell of expended ordnance, wood smoke, and cooked flesh mixed with human excrement and the puke of partially digested food released from sliced entrails.

A mist of fire-vaporized liquid droplets of human fat puffed across Lewis's body, condensed, leaving an oily coating on his fatigues and the exposed skin of arms and cheeks. Their boots and clothes would stink of this place no matter how often laundered.

The body he stood on jerked and writhed. Completely by nervous reflex, the lieutenant's .45 came up and fired into a preteen boy's bloody face. Lewis sickened, bent over, and added his stomach's contribution to the massacre. In the background, came the involuntary cries of NVA wounded between bursts of machine gunfire.

He heard George shriek. Death in the macaque's world came quickly and didn't hang around to sicken the survivors. Members of the troop vanished in the jaws of leopards or the claws of black eagles.

The monkey jerked the leash free, ran, and leaped over the heaped dead, finally disappearing into the surrounding woods. Their good luck mascot had deserted.

Poems from *Near Death/Near Life*
Published by Prolific Press in 2015.

KILL-ZONE REQUIEM

We wade through jungle shadows. Sweat drips
off our tiger-striped fatigues to wet red Asian soil.
Boots scuff, release fermented biting odors.
Butterflies blink wing eyes, shimmy dragon tails.

Insects in droning click-bodied clouds flutter,
nip, creep. Saw-toothed leaves and vine thorns
scar our necks and arms. The clack of hornbills,

the chortle of long-tail macaques set the tempo.
The bass drum whump of mortars firing slaps
our cheeks. Explosions shake triple canopy trees

their creaking limbs a pizzicato of violin and cello.
Bodies crazy-dance to the brass cymbal screech
of slicing shrapnel. We hear the tremolo drumstick

smack of jacketed bullets pierce canvas, cloth,
flesh. The splintered oboe thunk-grunt of metal

163

embedding in wood creates jittering chords.

Smoke-curdled air quivers with the clarinet warble
of blunt-nosed ricochets. We the dying give up
a final fugue of voices. Jumbled echoes fade,
weep off elephant grass, strangling fig, twisted lianas.

Flor de la Luna II

A la luz de las antorchas,
dedos chasquean las castañuelas,
faldas rizadas escarlatas,
remolinan alrededor de las piernas jóvenes,
al ritmo del Flamenco.

Las guitarras gime en el jardin,
y su calma agita con su caricia
hombros desnudos.

Pruebo la fragancia de ella
como pétalos color rosa en mi lengua.

Las flores se abren, se inclinan para
estar cerca de nosotros.
Su pelo se ajita en el aire.

Las caderas se sacuden cerca – los ojos
negros fuerzan mi corazón temblar.

De ella vienen las almas delicadas
de mujeres. De la luna es ella.

ABOUT THE AUTHOR

DENNIS MAULSBY is a retired bank president living in Ames, Iowa with his wife Ruth, a retired legal secretary, and his dog Charlie, a retired CIA operative. A son and grandson live in the Pacific Northwest. His poems and short stories have appeared in numerous literary journals and anthologies, including *The North American Review*, *Mainstreet Rag*, *The Hawai'i Pacific Review*, *The Briarcliff Review* (Pushcart nomination), and on National Public Radio's *Themes & Variations*. Some of his poems have been set to classical music and may be heard at his website: www.dennismaulsby.com.

His Vietnam War poetry book, *Remembering Willie*, won silver medal book awards from two national veterans' organizations. His book of poetry, *Near Death/Near Life*, and a book of short stories, *Free Fire Zone*, both published by Prolific Press, won a gold medal and a silver medal respectively from the Military Writers Society of America. Maulsby is a past president (2012 – 2014) of the Iowa Poetry Association.

The House de Gracie is his second book published with NeoLeaf Press. His first NeoLeaf Press publication, the American Fiction Award finalist *Winterset: Short Stories of Pixies, Demons and Fiends*, was released in 2019 and became their best seller for that year.

www.ingramcontent.com/pod-product-compliance
Lightning Source LLC
Chambersburg PA
CBHW051959220626
47052CB00004B/1013